Broken Ballads

Book One in the Stormy Skies Series

by

Katie Jane Newman

Dedicated to Amanda

Who wrote me a song, and sang it to me, when the skies went grey. One day she will appreciate boy bands as much as I do!

Special Thanks to

My group of amazing test readers, whose feedback and suggestions made this book a reality. Thank you, ladies, you ROCK x

Broken

(of a person) having given up all hope; despairing

Ballad

A slow, sentimental song or poem that tells a story.

Five Years Ago

Jonny

They haven't stopped chanting my name.

Three hundred thousand people roaring in unison – *Jonny, Jonny, Jonny, Jonny...* I've given them two hours, twenty-five songs, sweat and tears, but they still want more. The sound is thunderous, neanderthal, the one voice, made from so many, rings in my ears, stirring up my blood until it beats along with them. *One more song, one more song, one more song* replaces *Jonny.*

The exhaustion evaporates. Fuck it, they can have one more song. They have can have ten more songs. They can have as many songs as I can sing until my voice gives up. The bodies in the stadium send the electric atmosphere surging backstage, burning me with a fire that I've waited my entire life to feel. It's the brightest light, sizzling everything in its molten path until I'm vibrating with a raw, pure energy. This is it. This is *the* moment. My moment. Mine.

I throw a shot of whiskey down my throat and roll my shoulders. Never in my wildest dreams did I ever imagine that my fortieth birthday would be like this. Fronting the biggest show on earth. A show that has simultaneously been broadcast around the world – a birthday gift from me to those who couldn't get tickets. Nothing can ruin this moment. Nothing. I've made it. Against the odds. Little John Jones has been finally forgotten, instead I'm Jonny Raven, superstar, with the world at my feet - the world that is screaming for me. My musicians are depleted, most of them are collapsed on various sofas dotted around the huge room backstage, bottles in hand, but I don't care, I'll go out alone. The fans came for me. They will have me.

"Jonny?" Freddie, my manager comes into view.

6

"I'm going back out." I tell him stretching my neck from left to right.

"I'm not sure the band will want that." Freddie says, looking around at them, their faces drawn with fatigue.

"I'll do it on my own. It's fine."

"You don't want the night to end, huh?" He grins at me, pride flashing in his pale blue eyes.

"Can you hear them, Fred? It's insane! This is bigger than either of us could have ever imagined. It's un-fucking-believable!" I pick up an empty glass and pour a shot of whiskey into it, and top up mine, handing the fresh one to Freddie. "We've done it! The greatest fucking night in music ever…"

"Happy birthday, Mate! What a celebration! How does it feel to know that you've beaten all the names that came before, and that there is no way you'll be matched by anyone that follows. We're waiting for the viewing figures but even without them, you've done it! You've earned your place in the record books!" Freddie raises his glass to me, and I chink mine against his. The noise of the crowd is getting louder. They don't want to wait any more. The chanting has become feral and hungry. They want me. I want them. "To us! To you! Jonny Raven, superstar…"

"Thanks! I couldn't have done it without you, Fred."

Freddie knocks back his drink. "I'm proud of you mate! You said you'd do it, and you have!"

"The power of belief!" I stoop to pick up my guitar. "Wish me luck!"

"You don't need any more luck, Jonny." He stops me as I start to walk off. "Before you go back out, you've got a visitor waiting in the bar, can you just pop in..."

"Who? I'm not scheduled to see anyone, all the meet and greets have been done."

"It's not a fan, it's your dad. He said he lost his pass…"

The guitar is forgotten, and the whiskey glass falls from my hand. I watch it smash into glinting splinters across the wooden floor, the drink spreading into long amber strings. "What?" I whisper, my voice cracking into the broken sound I used to know. Long ago. When I had no power, no name and no hope. I cough. "How did he get backstage? Who the fuck let him in?"

Fred looks shocked. He waves at someone to clear up the mess. "Slight over-drama there, Jon, it's your dad, not a fucking stalker…"

"Who let him in?" I hiss, balling my hands so tightly into fists that the nails cut into my palms. The heat that I've been basking in has been replaced by an icy coldness and with it is the all too familiar fear that grips my throat, tightening its hold until I can't breathe. I pull at my neck with a shaking hand and feel the world begin to spin.

"Security did. Chelsea okayed it. What's the matter, you look like you've seen a ghost…"

"Get him the fuck out of here, Fred." Freddie doesn't move. "I said, GET HIM OUT."

"Alright mate, alright, calm down. I'll have him shown out." Fred waves at an assistant and when she reaches him, he leans in to say something into her ear. She gives me a strange look but nods before crossing the room to the door at the back. Fred gives me a beaming grin, which doesn't reach his eyes, and says "come on Jon, your adoring crowd wants you."

I can't do it. I can't go back out. I can't sing. I don't remember the words, or the songs. I can't do what they want me to do because I'm not Jonny Raven, it's all a lie. I'm no one, nothing, a waste of space, a disappointment. I'm *that fucking kid.* The world swims in front of my eyes and all I can hear is the slow, anguished thump of my breaking heart.

"There you are darling," Chelsea, my wife, sashays in and behind her...

"Hello son, it's been a while."

Present Day

Friday

Jonny

I wasn't planning on drinking today, but as days go, it's a fucking bad one.

"You're nearly broke, Jonny."

"Am I? Are you sure? You've said that numerous times over the years."

My accountant sighs and speaks slowly, as though explaining something to a small child. "I'm not joking, Jonny. This is serious. Really, really serious. Unless you somehow magic your missing money out of its secret hideaway, and fast, you won't even be able to keep your hotel."

"So, it's bad then," I say thinking that losing the hotel wouldn't necessarily be the worst thing.

I'm sure he mumbles *for fuck's sake* under his breath before he snaps. "Yes! Very bad. You'll be homeless."

I sigh and lift the glass back to my lips. Two decades of superstardom and nothing to show for it apart from a hotel located so far in the depths of Cornwall that most people have no idea the place even exists. The hotel inspectors tell me it could be spectacular, a luxury hotel to rival even the most exclusive destinations, but to me, it's just another noose to hang myself with. I groan. I fucking hate it, and if I could sell it, I would, but no one wants it. It may be the only place I can call home these days - everything else got sold to pay the bills - but I can never imagine ever being happy here. So far, it's brought nothing but misery.

I bought it after a riotous night out, when I was so inebriated that buying a hotel seemed like a good idea. All things seem like a good idea when you're drunk. Sober, and nearly broke, it's different. I still don't know what I was thinking. Why the fuck did I want a hotel in Cornwall? I certainly don't now but I can't sell it because no one wants to take it off my hands and end up stuck in the arse end of nowhereville.

It pays its way, but only just. I leave the management of it to the staff, and I stay up here, in my suite, out of the way. Most of the time, no one even knows I'm here.

If only the whiskey would help me truly forget it all. That it could somehow permanently erase the memories of my former glory days when I had the world in the palm of my hand and more money than I could count. In those days anything I wished for, I had.

Now my only wish is that I don't wake up.

I fought all my life to be someone, to lay the ghosts of my shit past to rest and to make sure that my daughter never had to feel anything like I felt when I was a child. Aria's amazing but I'm failing her just as much as I was failed, and it makes me sick.

"If you can stop Chelsea spending everything you have, you'll be able to pay Aria's school fees until she takes her A-Levels, and you can still pay Susie's alimony. But you have to cut up Chelsea's credit cards, that's the first thing to do if you want financial survival."

My flaky wife's one true love is shopping, and she spends as much as she can and as fast as possible. Her credit card bills are insane and when I ask her to stop using them, she throws my failure at me. *You're a drunk. You're disgusting. You're not the man I married...*I want to yell back, tell her she's lying - but it's all true. Every single word.

"Jonny, have you read my report?" The accountant asks.

"Of course."

I haven't, and he knows it. The report lies discarded on the floor. The papers are wet where they soaked up some liquid. Probably whiskey. It's my best friend these days.

"You need to read it Jonny, before things get worse."

"How can things possibly get worse?" I give a curt goodbye and knock the whiskey back in one as my gaze falls onto the magazine, staring up at me from on the coffee table. There is an old photo of me on the cover, guitar in hand. It's the 'me' I remember being, but that person is long gone. I don't know who thought it appropriate to leave it outside my suite. I half expected it to have been Chelsea, she likes giving me reminders of the past when she can, but it wasn't posted, and she doesn't come down to Cornwall if she can help it. Besides, it would have been too much effort for her to arrange for it to be left somewhere for me to see. Chelsea doesn't like effort any more than she likes Cornwall.

I haven't read the magazine. I don't need to, but it taunts me from the table and the headline screams loudly enough that I can hear it from wherever I stand. *The Lost Generation of Rock* and the by-lines - *forgotten, irrelevant, whatever happened to* – are salt in the festering wounds.

I pour another glass of whiskey. Anything to drown it all out. Down in one. Feeling the burn as the amber liquid hits the back of my throat. Pour another, then another and another until everything is a blur. Jonny Raven - Broke. Drunk. Lost. Forgotten. Somewhere, beyond my reach, there are the faint stirrings of memories, of lights, of rapture, of words pouring from my fingers, but I can't catch them. Too far away. Irrelevant now.

I slam the glass down on the table where it splinters. Fuck. I use the magazine to push the shards to one side and take another glass from the tray in the centre of the table, pouring more from the bottle. Most of it slops onto the wood but I drink what the glass holds. Down in one. Another glass. Down in one. Another, and another and

14

another until I spill the next refill because I can't coordinate my actions. Drip, drip onto the floor. Carefully I put the bottle to my lips. Ahhh, the darkness is coming. This time, perhaps I won't wake up. Perhaps they'll forget I'm here. Perhaps no one will come. I'm irrelevant, why would they? The accountant will pay the bills until there is no money left. The guests won't know there is a decomposing nobody in the penthouse. They won't care. They don't know who I am anyway.

I drop the bottle and it crashes onto the finance papers. I watch as they soak up the liquid, the black type blurring. The paper swells. I strike a match and drop it onto the reports. I expect a fire. There is nothing. The flame burns out. Like me. Burnt out. No fire.

I can hear laughter coming from the gardens below. I used to laugh. Once upon a time. When I knew who I was. I don't know when I last laughed. Nothing is funny anymore. It's all fucked up and the blackness is suffocating. I'm drowning. I take some long gulps of whiskey and splutter. My eyes sting, it comes out my nose and I dribble. Fucking dribble. Like an old, forgotten man. I am forgotten. Not old, not yet, but I feel it.

One moment was all it took to sink into the abyss. Chelsea would say it was the drink, that the moment I had dreaded for thirty-three years was no big deal, that I was just lazy and pathetic. Of course, she would say it was my fault. Maybe she's right, maybe it was me. I should have been stronger. I let it happen. I didn't stand up for myself. I was scared. Still just a terrified child sobbing in the corner of a filthy room. Maybe it is my fault that I'm lost in the suffocating darkness. Maybe I am just a big mistake. *Should never have been born. Fucking piece of shit.* I spill whiskey down my tee-shirt. I'm disgusting. When did I become so disgusting? *No longer relevant.*

Broken memories of glory days. I thought it would last forever but life chewed me up and spat me out. *You're disgusting.* Am I? Is this really me? *You're a drunk.* I didn't used to be. *All that talent, wasted.* Wasted. Waster. Fucking wasted. I slop more whiskey down my shirt as I try to lift the bottle to my mouth. I am nothing. A nobody. A broke, broken, wasted, drunk. *Disgusting.* One more mouthful then oblivion comes.

Saturday

Jonny

"It's a fucking reality show, don't you watch TV? You must do, you're doing fuck all..."

"Fred..."

"Hear me out, Jon," my manager interrupts me quickly. Too quickly. It makes my brain rattle. "You have no money because that fucking idiot bimbo you married has spent it all. I mean, how the fuck did she spend it?" He doesn't wait for me to answer because he knows as well as I do that she spent it because it gets my attention. Also, she hasn't spent all of it, I have a lot of money, I just don't know where I put it and my accountant is still waiting for me to work out where it's hidden. "Let's face it, Jonny, no one knows who you are anymore and those that do, think you're dead. It's a good opportunity to make some quick cash. Kids love that reality shit. Middle-agers love that shit and it's not even real! They'll watch it, remember you and buy compact fucking discs because they're old school. The kids will look you up on some fucking music site they all subscribe to, and BAM you'll be back."

The BAM is too enthusiastic, and it hurts my head. I move and the empty whiskey bottle falls off the sofa onto the piles of paper that I still haven't read. They're illegible now and the papers have merged into one soggy mess of spilled alcohol. I should care but I don't. When did I stop caring? When was the last time I shaved, or showered? Or eaten? There are plates of untouched food dotted around the suite, attracting flies, but no one has cleared my rooms in weeks, and I've not asked housekeeping. I don't care enough. I've just self-medicated on cheap alcohol. I am revolting.

I didn't used to be. But the bloated, drunken mess I've become isn't worthy of thought. Of care. Of anything. I'm irrelevant and the voice inside my head won't let up.

"Look Jonny," Freddie sighs and speaks slowly. "You have to do something. You can't lie around in the back of beyond not seeing anyone and not doing anything. It's making me fucking miserable so I can't image what it's doing to you..."

"I'm fine."

"Really? I've got to be honest, Jonny, you don't sound fine. I spoke to the dopey bird on the reception desk, and she said that they've not seen you for days. You could be dead for all they know."

"I am dead."

Freddie groans. "Look mate," he blows a long breath out, "I didn't want to say this but unless you start making money, we aren't going to be able to represent you anymore. Trying to find shit for you takes too much time and you're just not earning your keep. I'm sorry Jon, it's hard to say this to you, we've been friends for years, and I've always had your back, but we have a big client list, and I don't have the time to keep fighting your corner. I'm so sorry mate. I've fought for you, feeling sure this is just a blip, but the partners have come to a decision that we won't be able to offer you representation if you don't make it pay."

"So, what are you saying? I do some shit show where people have to fucking google me, or you'll drop me?"

"It's one hundred grand, it's a start. It's more than the other has-beens..." He stops and I can hear his horror at the slip.

The pause is just too long. "Bye Freddie." I say eventually and cancel the call.

Well. Fuck. Is that it? After twenty-five years? It's all over? Just like that?

19

I feel sick. Through it all Freddie has been my right-hand man. Guiding. Making decisions. Bringing out the best in me. Hiding the worst. Dragging me from women's beds. Sending me to rehab. Keeping it all quiet. Paying people who needed paying. I couldn't take a shit without Freddie's approval. Now he's gone and the final piece of wall crumbles. There is nothing left. The old me. The old life. It's gone.

All I have left is the pain. It rips through me tearing my insides apart. I wrap my arms around my stomach to hold it all together but the icy knife slashes me and I feel my body smashing onto the floor, the empty bottle breaking under me.

Then I cry.

I fucking cry.

And blood spills.

And there is pain.

So much pain.

Molly

"Happy birthday to you. Happy birthday to you, happy birthday dear Molly, happy birthday to you." Paul, my boyfriend looks really pleased with himself. He's filled the room with balloons, and it seems that everyone I've ever met is singing at me.

I hate surprises, especially surprise parties. I was supposed to be having dinner with Paul, my parents, my best friend Ella, and her boyfriend, and now I'm holding a glass of something sparkly and have slapped on smile so big that my cheeks are aching. God, I'm tired. Work has been crazy, which I'm thankful for, but starting my own business has left me feeling completely drained. A party is the last thing I need.

Today I turned thirty. It feels so old. It could have almost been yesterday that I met Paul, but we've been in a relationship for eleven years and I don't know where the time has gone. Eleven years with a man who knows that I hate surprises. He's never done anything like this before. I don't know why he has now. I hate myself for being so ungrateful, but I can't help it. This is my worst nightmare. Paul knows that.

We were going to my most favourite oriental restaurant in Bath. I'd already planned my menu choices and spent all day drooling at the thought but now I'm faced with chicken dippers and non-descript meat on skewers. I know I'm being horrible. It's a kind thing that he's done, but the room is full of people in my contacts list, and most of them are not friends. Not real friends. Just people I know. On the table in the corner of the room is a mound of presents and Paul is standing by them, pint in hand, grinning at me like the cat who go the cream. I feel terrible for not being more *yay* about the party. When I wasn't paying attention, something changed, and this is another reminder that my feelings about him aren't the same. I don't know what to do about it. We've been together so long that I can't remember who I was before him. He was supposed to just be a one-night stand after a tequila party at the student union, but somehow, we've lasted longer than anyone thought we would. He says he loves me, that he's in love with me, but yesterday the thought popped into my head that it was nothing more than habit, and now I can't stop thinking about it. Habit. Is that what we are? Just walking the path everyone expects us to, without even being aware of our footsteps.

I suppose I love him, he's familiar, comfortable but 'in love', no, I don't think I am anymore, and I wonder if it would be hard to let go of 'us'. We're *Molly and Paul.* Our uni friends call us Polly, they think it's funny. I did once. Back in the days where we could barely get out of bed to go to lectures. The sex was great. Not mind-blowing, but great. Now it's perfunctory and infrequent. It's me. I'm at fault. I'm tired all the time, long hours and demanding clients. Paul hates it. Hates my job. Hates that it gets more attention than he does. *When are you going to get a proper job Moll?* I thought I had finally had it all – great boyfriend, amazing new career. Maybe it was just wishful thinking. I wonder when things changed.

He's still grinning, and my fake smile gets wider. There is an envelope in his hand. I was panicking about a ring but an envelope I can cope with. Envelopes aren't scary. It's probably a spa weekend, I love those. He would do something like that, treat Ella and me to a spa weekend. He's kind like that. Paul is great, everyone thinks so.

"Molly, there were times I didn't think either of us would make thirty." My uni friends cackle, everyone who isn't in on the joke laughs politely. He's referring to the bad diet and endless drinking of our early twenties. "But we did, and now we're all here to celebrate you. Molly Bloom, business owner, trashy tv lover and my better half." Oh god, he's going for it, please no ring, please no ring. "You're hard to buy for these days, but…" Paul pauses dramatically and there is a collective intact of breath. "Happy birthday Molly." He hands me the envelope and I tentatively feel it. Phew, no ring. Everyone waits expectantly.

I turn up the smile until my face threatens to crack and open the envelope. Inside is a thick card, embossed with a logo and I have high hopes for a really luxurious spa weekend. I pull out the card and it takes everything to have to keep the smile on my face. A cooking course. In Cornwall.

"What is it?" Someone asks. I have to fight to stop the tears. They're behind my eyes, prickling and burning. Paul is looking delighted. I think I would have preferred the ring.

"Wow." I utter eventually.

"She's overwhelmed." Someone else says and I nod.

"Wow." I repeat myself but I don't know what else to say. Paul is waiting for a grand thank you and for me to fall squealing with delight into his arms, but I can't make myself speak. Or move.

"I've bought her a cooking course in Cornwall." Paul looks delighted. I catch Ella's eye. She looks as shocked as I feel.

"No more microwave meals for you, Paul. Nice one!" It's one of Paul's friends, Simon. He's a dick.

Paul laughs. "I'm set for cordon bleu dinners for the rest of my life," he says. "It's with Chef Patron Brewster, he does really fancy cooking, has a restaurant in London that all the celebs go to. It's right up Molly's street." It's nowhere near my street. It's the complete opposite of my street.

Paul knows that I hate fancy food and I really hate cooking. I'm shocked that he would gift me something like that and I'm gutted that I hate my present. I've never hated anything he's bought me before. I don't dare look at Ella because then I'll cry and that would be awful. Still, a few days in Cornwall would be good. I could do with a break. Work has been relentless, for which I'm so grateful, it could have been so much worse. Being made redundant from the forensic accounting firm I'd been working at since I graduated has been a blessing but I'm tired. Some sea air and some time to plan, and a break from my life, is just what I need. No one need know that I didn't attend the course.

"And the best bit," Paul continues to his adoring crowd, "is that there is a webcam so we can watch Molly hard at work."

Shit.

Sunday

Molly

I'm sober when I get into bed. Paul is snoring, face down in his pillow with drool dampening the fabric. He smells of beer and cheap rum, and his t-shirt is sticking to his sweaty back. I used to love watching him sleep. Paul is really handsome, in a preppy sort of way, with a mop of dark blond hair and bright blue eyes. When we met, I couldn't get enough of him - funny, gorgeous, fit, ambitious, generous – Paul had it all and for all our friends, and the followers of his vlog, he still does. He is a good person most of the time, so why isn't it enough? What's wrong with me?

I lie in the dark trying to make sense of what I no longer feel. Where has it gone? Paul and I have always been the right fit. We laugh at the same things, watch the same movies, enjoy the same life, so why has it changed? The change came so quickly that I didn't see it coming. Until today. Why today?

What would I have done if it had been a ring? Said yes? Our relationship is a safe place, at least, it always has been. Tears form, stinging my eyes and there is a sadness that is overwhelming. I feel that everything is breaking, and I don't know how to fix it.

Paul jerks in his sleep and rolls towards me. His breath smells sour and his tongue, lolling on the side of his mouth, is filmy. My stomach twists with guilt as I look down at him. It's just not the same anymore and he's not noticed. Then the voice whispers *when has he ever really noticed you?*

I don't know when I fell asleep, but the sky had gotten light, and the birds were stirring. My eyes sting with fatigue as I wake. It's too early. I close my eyes again, but the damage has been done. I gently pull myself out from under Paul's arm and creep from the bedroom. The mound of birthday presents are on the floor by the sofa but I ignore them and wander into our tiny kitchen. My phone flashes with unread messages but I don't pick it up and instead I fill the kettle. Paul's voucher is on the side and while the kettle heats, I open it. Four days in Cornwall. Cooking. I want to feel cross, but instead I'm just sad. Sad that I can't be happy. Sad that everything feels broken.

I make a cup of strong tea and take it outside to our garden. It's the smallest space ever but we've filled it with pots and candles, so it looks really cosy. I love it usually but this morning it feels too crowded. I flop down into the seat and put the cup on the bistro table. Perhaps that's what it is, perhaps I just feel crowded.

I've given so much of myself to my new interior design business that maybe these feelings are just exhaustion. I love what I do, love the crazy days and the demanding clients, the unpredictable moments that I never had when I was tied to the office. I'm so blessed that it's going so well, but what I really need is a break, a few days where no one needs anything from me. Maybe Cornwall will do me some good. The whispered voice in my head says, *maybe you need a break from Paul.*

Jonny

"What the actual fuck has happened here?" I open a stinging eye to see Chelsea standing over me, her frozen face puce with fury. "You are disgusting. DISGUSTING." Her screech makes my ears bleed.

"It's not what you think…" My tongue clicks against the dry roof of my mouth.

"No? Are you sure about that?" She sweeps her arm in the general direction of the filth I've been living in and pulls her cardigan tighter around her, as though she'll catch something unspeakable. "It looks to me that it's everything I think it is…"

"Freddie dumped me"

"I'm not surprised."

"Thanks," I mutter pushing myself up from the floor. There is glass below me, some of which has embedded into my torso. It hurts. Badly.

"Oh my God, Jonny, there's blood everywhere!"

"It's not as bad as it looks." I say, crossing an arm under my ribs. I'm lying. It hurts like hell. I shuffle like an old man to the bathroom and slam the door behind me. It's been days, maybe weeks, since I last looked in the mirror, but in the cold light of day, there is no escape. I grip the edge of the sink and take a deep breath. I don't want to look. I don't even know who I am anymore. My identity has been torn to shreds and everything that made me *me* has been ripped away. Maybe Chelsea is right, maybe I am just a disgusting has-been drunk with nothing to offer the world. Maybe she can do better. I take a couple of deep breaths in, and my rib cage burns.

Then I look.

The sight looking back at me is horrific. My hair is matted and limp with grease, and the beard that covers my jaw is coarse and dull. My skin is grey, sickly looking, as though my hermit existence has drained me of colour and left nothing behind but death. I lock eyes with myself. They're red, dry and I can no longer see my soul. I am gone. There isn't anything there that I recognise.

I take a deep breath in, wincing as pain ricochets through my ribs and sends fire to the cuts. Slowly I tug the tee-shirt over my head, grimacing at the stench that comes from under my armpits. What a catch. What a fucking catch. Then I'm swamped with memories so clear that I have to grip onto the sink to keep upright. Karma is taunting me. Showing me all that I was and all that I lost. Bright lights. Chants. Sounds. Life. I'm not prepared for the images to bombard my head in such glorious technicolour. *Go away. Leave me alone.* Then the pictures fade and I feel so fucking lost that I can't breathe and all I can see in the mirror is hungover, sweaty, filthy me. My torso is covered in dried blood, looking as though I've been slashed and sticking out from the cuts are shards of the broken bottle. Screwing my face up against the pain, I pull them out with the tweezers I find in the vanity unit. The cuts bleed. Slowly, I cross to the shower and turn it on, letting the water heat up before standing under it. She can't hear me cry in here. The water turns red. The grief of a life lost wells up until I slump unto the corner of the shower, pulling my legs up and cry until there are no tears left.

Irrelevant.

Drunk.

A broken broke drunk.

You disgust me.

Oh well, Chelsea, you don't need to worry, I disgust me more.

✱✱✱

Chelsea is sitting on the sofa, legs up, magazines covering the coffee table. She doesn't look at me as I walk into the room. I can't remember when she ever did look at me as though she could actually see *me,* the real me. It was my name she fell in love with and the status and glory of being someone by association. It was never love. She has never loved me. I was a means to an end. A way out of the factory job and the life of hardship that she feared. Chelsea needs to be somebody and at the beginning of our marriage I made it possible for her to have everything she desired – money, fame, glory – but when the spotlight faded, anything she felt for me faded too. She was never going to be the person to help me back to the light. She doesn't care that I lost everything that mattered, she just cares about the status she has lost.

I try and see the Chelsea I married, but she is so different now. Back then she was really pretty, all bouncing curls and big blue eyes. Then she met her surgeon. *You look amazing,* they all said as her soft, ripe breasts were inflated by silicone. She didn't. I hated her new breasts. Then it was her lips and the injections that turned her perfect pout into swollen and hard lumps.

She's eighteen years younger than me, but we both look a mess.

"I wasn't expecting you." I said lightly. It took effort to be light.

"Why?" She flicked the page of the magazine she was reading. "You are my husband." Chelsea eyed me. "Well, you used to be."

"Why are you such a bitch?"

"Why are you such a waster?" She snaps back. "And just so you know, I spoke to the accountant. We're skint. You need to make some money." She paused. "I also

30

spoke to Freddie. The reality show sounds good. I love that show…"

"I don't want to do it."

"You're broke. That makes me broke. I don't like being broke."

"Get a job then." I snapped.

Chelsea's eyes narrow until they're mere slits. The rest of her face doesn't move but I can feel the simmering anger radiating from her. Her brain is ticking over, trying to find something disparaging to say but she's not quick enough. Instead, she just huffs and goes back to her magazine. "You need to clear up this shit tip. Can't a maid come in? That's what you pay them for."

"I'll do it."

"Do it then." Chelsea snaps. "But I'll have vodka and tonic before you do."

"It's too early." I don't know why I said it.

She gestures at the empty and broken bottles that litter the room. "That doesn't appear to stop you."

She's right. It doesn't but even so, I don't make her the drink. Instead, I collect the bin from the bathroom, wincing as the small movement pulls at the cuts, and set it in the middle of the coffee table. Chelsea idly watches me as I scrape forgotten plates of food into the bin and set the crockery in a pile.

"What's the point of having staff if you do it yourself?" She asks.

Because enough people find me disgusting. "They have work to do." They don't, not really. The hotel, despite its prime beach location, isn't doing as much business as it should. My name doesn't sell it, and the interior is tired, sad and desperate for a complete change. Like me really. I look at Chelsea. She is taking selfies, ready to upload, the perfect image for a fake reality. She wants to be someone. It's a need. No discernible talent but a longing to be famous, as though fame makes everything ok. As though it can erase the past and recreate something from the ashes.

My chest tightens and sucks the breath from me. I used to be someone, for a moment it wiped out the life I wanted to forget, but the demons hung on tightly and there has never been anyone to help me banish them. If only the words would come, if only I could hear the music, then maybe it would be different. Maybe the bright lights would shine again because the darkness I'm lost in is suffocating. Bleak. It's an engulfing black fog that locked me away in a hellish prison and, even five years later, I cannot see a way out.

Chelsea being here has just made everything worse.

"Seems to me they do very little." She says, wrinkling her nose. "The whole place stinks. Maybe, now I'm here, I should get them to actually do their job? The only way to make any money is this hotel, and you sitting up here being a slob won't keep the bank account full."

"As I said, get a job."

"Don't be silly Jonny. I didn't..." She stops. What she wants to say is that she didn't marry me to have to get a job. I was the job. The stepping stone to being someone with influence, a celebrity famous for doing nothing apart from posting selfies and being 'seen'. It's no wonder she hates me. Nine years of marriage and so much money wasted, a mountain of bills and the pressure to be who I used to be. She wants that person. She doesn't want this one.

"Are you listening?" Chelsea snaps, throwing her magazine onto the coffee table.

"No." She doesn't like my honesty.

"I said that we should have a party, put the hotel on the map, get the London elite down here..."

"They wouldn't come."

"Well, try writing something and they would…"

"I don't want to go over this again, Chelsea." I say sharply. "You know I can't. Do you think I'm down here for the good of my health?"

She casts her eyes around the room. "You're definitely not down here for that. You shouldn't have sold the SoHo apartment…"

"Leave it alone, Chelsea."

"Just saying," Chelsea says, pulling a vape out of her bag and sucking on it. Plumes of smoke leave her inflated mouth. She looks ridiculous.

I scrape more plates, if only to avoid the cold silence. It takes me awhile. I've been living in squalor and there are mouldy plates littering most surfaces. Eventually they are all stacked alongside glasses and empty whisky bottles. It's shameful. I am ashamed. I put them on a tray and carry them down to the kitchen, taking the staff route. I'm relieved that I manage to avoid seeing anyone, but the relief doesn't last long.

"I've invited everyone." Chelsea says when I get back.

"Pardon?" My heart sinks. The last thing I want, or need, is a party filled with Chelsea's ridiculous friends. "I don't want a party. I didn't agree to a party. Chelsea, there isn't the money for a party."

"For fucks' sake Jonny, are you literally trying to ruin my life? It's bad enough that we have no London home anymore, and that you're down here in this shit pile festering like some fucking hobo," she paused and took in a big breath. "I'm living like a fucking poor person, Jonny – "the personalised Hermes bag on the table seems to glint at me – "and now you're saying we can't have a party." Chelsea's voice goes up an octave. "I'm dying of boredom. We are having a party, it's arranged, all my friends are coming so stop being a fucking skinflint."

33

"I don't like your friends."

"You don't have to like them. I couldn't give a shit if you like them or not, because I like them. They are influencers, Jonny, their endorsement could be just what this dump needs. Being poor doesn't suit me, so you have to do something."

Endorsements by fake wannabe celebrities isn't what I need. I don't want the pitying looks or the blank faces when my name is mentioned. I want someone to notice me. Find the real me who has been lost under the whiskey, self-revulsion and the complete disinterest of my wife. I should never have married her. I was too old, she was too young, it was never going to work.

"Did you know that they've written a magazine article about you?"

"I'm surprised you read it."

"I had planned to send it to you, but as I was coming down – "She rummages in her bag. "Look!" Chelsea is almost euphoric as she holds the magazine up. *"The Lost Generation of Rock.* I wanted to ring them and tell them that you're not lost, you're just doing fuck all in a skanky pit, but I didn't want anyone to know that my husband is a total loser."

"Why are you such a bitch?"

"Because I'm depressed, Jonny. This -" she gestures around the room, "is fucking depressing. It's time you manned-up and did something, so people don't think you're a no one."

"Imagine being married to a no one." I say wryly. "Oh, the shame…"

Then her phone rings.

I'm forgotten as Chelsea answers it. "Aurora, darling, it's been too long."

My torso burns as I go back to cleaning up. Chelsea is still talking on the phone, and I catch snippets as I move around the suite - a party, a celebrity, heading back to London, staying somewhere, facial, shoes – maybe I should just divorce her. It's a toxic marriage and we are no good for each other. It wouldn't take her long to find someone else to pick up the tabs. I'm surprised she hasn't already.

The ache for a whiskey is nearly as bad as the ache from the cuts. I ignore both and continue cleaning lost in my own thoughts until Chelsea interrupts.

"I'm going back to London." She says, pulling out the handle of her suitcase. "Can you pay my credit card balance now, because it's maxed."

I nod. "Did you drive?"

"Yes, I borrowed LaLa's Ferrari, he has two, didn't mind me using one. You don't think I'd be getting the train, did you?"

Who the fuck is LaLa?

The diamonds on her ring finger catch the light and throw rainbows onto her hand. She wanted the biggest, the brightest, the most expensive and she got them. She can keep them. By the time she finishes shopping it'll be the only thing of value left.

"Bye darling, I'll be back in a few days to get ready for our party. Maybe think about that reality show, it would be good for you. Love you." She doesn't love me, of that I am completely sure. Chelsea opens the suite door, blows me a kiss, and lets the door close behind her.

She has been here for an hour.

***

"Is the idiot there or has she gone?" My fifteen-year-old daughter asks during our Sunday afternoon call. "I saw on Instagram that she was going to Cornwall, then there was another picture of her in a Ferrari looking like a

35

total embarrassment and talking about cocktails in town, so I thought she was either talking shit or…"

"Aria!"

"What?" Aria askes with a false innocence ringing in her voice. "You know I love Chelsea, Dad!" She doesn't wait for me to comment. There is no love lost between my wife and my daughter which used to really bother me but these days, not so much. "You haven't forgotten that I'm coming to stay at half term, have you? Mum is going on a work trip with Luke, and I can't go to Grandma's because she's going on a cruise, so I'm afraid you're stuck with me. It's just the first week though so can Chelsea please not be there? Please?"

I've no idea when half term is. "It's unlikely that she will be. Why only the first week? Usually you come for both."

"Well, Dad." She says firmly, "if you bothered to read your emails and pay the invoice, you'll know that I'm going on an archaeology excursion to Egypt. Miss Langdon asked me to remind you that you've not paid it yet, and Mum says she can't pay it because you're behind in alimony. Grandma won't pay it because she's upgraded to the penthouse cabin or something, and my bank account has got a tenner in it, so sorry Dad, it's up to you."

"I'll pay it." I lean back in the chair and wince as the cuts on my stomach pull. The glass of water on the side table isn't as appealing as the whiskey on the bar, but if I'm ever going to straighten myself out, the drink has got to go.

"Now?"

"Well, not right this minute, but now-ish!"

"How now-ish are you talking Dad, because you haven't done it so far and Miss Langdon keeps asking me in front of the whole class…"

"I'll do it as soon as I'm off the phone."

"Thanks. You're the best!" Aria says cheerily. She doesn't pause for breath as she launches into a tirade of information about life at boarding school - her friends, the teachers who are having an affair and how she's getting on being hockey captain. I drink my water and listen. She is the apple of my eye, my feisty, sassy daughter, and somehow, she has turned out to be bright, sparky and grounded despite my hedonistic lifestyle and horrific fall from grace. It helps that her mother, Susie, is decent, and doesn't hate me for being a shit husband. We have a pretty good relationship for a divorced couple, especially given we were only married for a year before she'd had enough of me.

They all have enough of me in the end.

Susie is happy now, married to a nice but boring chap called Luke, with a normal, everyday sort of job. He's much better for her than I ever was, and he loves Aria so that makes him ok in my book. More ok than me.

I sigh.

"Dad, are you even listening?" Aria asks sharply.

"Yes."

"I don't think you were because I was telling you about Chelsea's Instagram posts and you said, 'lovely' when it isn't lovely at all. Honestly, Dad, I know I keep saying it, but she is a terrible person. She's always hanging off someone who isn't you, and posting it all over social media, which is so embarrassing especially as everyone at school follows her. She makes my skin itch. You need someone decent, but this time, I get to choose. You keep picking idiots because they're pretty, but I don't want a stepmother who goes out in knickers and tassels, because that's what idiot Chelsea wore last night to drape herself over some footballer. Bitchy Bonnie in year eleven showed me the pictures over breakfast this morning and then laughed with all her bitchy friends..."

"Sorry..."

"It's ok, I'll just hit her with my hockey stick next time she comes to practice."

"I'm not sure you should be doing that!"

"So, divorce Chelsea and then I won't have to! Everyone knows you're married to her, they must think you're ..."

"People don't know who I am these days, Aria, so they won't think anything!"

"Of course they know who you are because a magazine has come out practically dedicated to you! Most of the girls have stuck the cover up on their walls and keep telling me that you're a hot dad! Urgh it's so disgusting." I can almost hear her shudder and smile when I picture the look on her face. "Not that you're disgusting, I mean, you're really handsome and everything, Dad, but they're all crushing on you and it's weird. Although everyone has been streaming your albums so you might get rich again."

Perhaps Freddie was right, perhaps I should do that show.

"You should come back to London and live here again, and then I can hang out with you all the time, well, when I'm back from school obviously. At least in London there is a chance that you will actually meet the perfect woman who isn't an idiot like Chelsea, because you won't meet anyone stuck down there. Cornwall is nice but it's not like someone is going to just turn up on the doorstep. It would be great if you'd get back together with Mum, but I know that's not going to happen, so a nice person in London would be the next best thing."

"When did you get so grown up?" I ask her fondly.

"When you were living in Cornwall and not doing what you should be doing."

"Too much time has passed to do all those things again, Aria." I hear chatter in the background and her name being called.

"You could be great again, like before, you're so talented Dad." She pauses and I feel a knot of anguish so huge swell in my stomach and squeeze the breath from me. "Got to go, I've got drama club. Love you."

She's gone before I can return the sentiment.

I could murder a drink.

Molly

"Now drive carefully and ring me when you get there." It comes out like an instruction as Paul loads my case and a couple of files into the boot. "And don't forget to enjoy it. The course is one of the best, you'll have a great time."

I nod. Paul doesn't seem to notice my lack of enthusiasm or if he does, he doesn't care. A week is a long time to be away from work, especially a business as young as mine and I feel a gripping anxiety when I think about it. I've had to rearrange meetings in London with insanely wealthy prospective clients, all for a poxy cooking course in the depths of Cornwall. I want to tell him that I'd rather not go, that the meetings need to take precedence, but he looks so excited for me, and so pleased with his choice of gift, that the words won't come.

I wait for the pang that I'll miss him.

It doesn't come either.

The voice in my head whispers quietly to me, telling me everything I'm trying to ignore. A break will be good. It will give me time to think. Perhaps Paul and I just need enough space to miss each other, and then maybe we can find our way back. *Or maybe not. Maybe there is something more for you.*

"Do you have your voucher?" Paul asks.

"Yes, it's in the case."

"And the hotel is programmed into your sat nav?"

"Yes." He did it. He's done all of it.

"Then you'd best be on your way."

Suddenly I feel as though Paul wants me out of the way. "What will you be doing this week?" I ask him, opening the car door.

40

He doesn't meet my eye. "I've got the lads coming over on Wednesday for the match and some work meetings. Not much."

There never is much these days. Our social life used to be crazy, but I can't remember the last time we went out. I can't remember the last time we did anything.

I pull my seatbelt around me and put the key in the ignition. "Sounds like a good week."

"Not as good as the one you'll have." Paul says smiling. "Just be safe."

I nod. There isn't a kiss. He closes the door and I turn the key. When was the last kiss?

I pull away from the house, on my way to a cooking course. I'm thirty. There wasn't a kiss. There was nothing at all.

***

The hotel is basic, and my view is the wall of the next-door property. I had a romantic vision of a gothic Cornish property on the beach where I could take long walks and feel the sea breeze, instead I'm staying in a no-frills hotel in the centre of town. Then I feel horribly ungrateful. I'm not this person - this whiny, miserable, disappointed person. It feels as though I've hit a midlife crisis a decade early and I don't know how to shake myself out of it. I put the kettle on and open one of the plastic-wrapped biscuits, staring out of the window at the wall as I nibble it. It's started to rain, and the plops are hitting something in the alley below making a tap-tap sound.

Once the kettle has boiled, I make tea and sit on the bed, turning the tv on. Only a couple of channels work so I watch an ancient re-run of an eighties sit-com which isn't funny and work through some emails. I schedule appointments, phone my mum, and then make my way down to the street. There is a chain pub a couple of doors up, so I head there and order a glass of wine, which tastes more like sweet vinegar, and a meal.

In the booth opposite me are a group of men, around my age, wearing football shirts with a table full of empty glasses. They're laughing at something one of them has said, and I find the edges of my mouth start to curl upwards. Their uncontrollable mirth is catching, and I giggle.

The laughter quietens and the men go back to their drinks, one of them shouting across to the bar tender to 'put the match on, mate,' and a cheer goes up when the channel gets changed. I sip at the vinegar in my glass and pick up a discarded magazine left on the table. The headline reads *The Lost Generation of Rock* and inside, pictures and stories about the bad boys of music – women, drink, drugs, excess – and the decline that followed. It makes sad reading. I pause over the photo of the rock star on the cover and can't make my eyes move away from the page.

There is something about him that keeps my gaze fixed so tightly that I barely blink. It may be his eyes - a strange silver colour, almost wolf-like, or the thick chestnut hair that is cropped close to his head, or the shadow that covers the rugged chin. Perhaps I just recognise the lost look because it's the same look that I seem to have every single time I look in the mirror.

I don't know why I feel so lost inside the life I have. From the outside, it's a great – lovely home, lovely couple, great jobs, healthy bank accounts – absolutely nothing to complain about on the surface, but underneath, where the truth sits it's harder to pretend that everything is perfect. We no longer have any shared interests, and we no longer laugh at the silly things. Paul doesn't make me a coffee in the morning these days. Since I've been working from home, I hardly see him, even though we are both there almost every day. It's all gone wrong. We've gone wrong. I didn't notice for a while but now I see it all too clearly. It's why I didn't want the ring. I still don't know what I would have done if it had been a ring.

I find myself suddenly longing for the days when all Paul and I did was laugh. For all those years when we knew each other inside out and held each other's hopes and dreams in our hands tightly. I have always supported Paul's ambitions but him supporting mine feels like a lifetime ago. He's so resentful now that I don't even talk about my work, I keep quiet, pretending that I can't feel my power fade.

I pick up the magazine and look again at the handsome rock star. He had his dream job and lost it all. How much did he have to give up getting to the top, and how hard must the fall have been? I've got my dream job now, but I'm sacrificing so much for it that I don't know if the fight is worth it. *Always,* the voice says, *it is always worth it.* Then I get the strange feeling again and the voice whispers, *there is something out there waiting for you.*

The waitress brings over my food and I eat it while scanning social media. It's the way I've been marketing my business, and the constant need for interesting content has become a full-time job. Paul often complains that I am on my phone too much, and he's right. Perhaps the problems we have are because of me, because of the business that has taken over my life. Maybe it's me that needs to change, not us.

I pop a few posts onto my social pages and yawn. I'm tired. I've been tired since I lost my job and started my interior design business. It was supposed to be a bit of fun, an Instagram page that focused on the home improvements and the decorating I did while job hunting, and then it exploded. Questions, comments, emails – it was relentless as my style seemed to inspire others and a business was born. My bank account has never been so healthy. Zoom calls with clients who walk me around their stately piles or their city flats with the most fashionable postcodes, fill my days. Vision boards whizz back and forth via email and my diary is filled with appointments. I am both grateful and worn out.

Paul hates it.

He hates my new job, finds it invasive and complains that it takes all my time, and that he gets none. Did I do it on purpose, to hide from the problems or did it create the problems that I now hide from? I lay my phone on the table face down and stare out of the window where the rain is falling harder, hitting the glass with a clatter.

"It's going to get worse," one of the men on the other table says when he notices me looking at the grey evening. "The forecast says it's going to be the worst rain for years. Tourists are being told not to come, I guess you didn't get that message?"

"No!" My heart sinks. "How much rain are they talking?"

"A years' worth over a couple of days. How long are you here for?" He asks.

"I'm here for this week. I'm going to a cooking course with Chef Patron Brewster."

"Pompous prick," one of the others says. "He claims to be a Cornish chef but is never here. London can keep him. No one likes him around here, he drives in, creates fuss and goes again. Wanker. Plus, his food is shit. Give me pie and chips any day." He pats his enormous belly and laughs. "I'm sure his course is great, but you shouldn't really be here. The rain will stop you leaving if it's as heavy as they say it will be."

The waitress brings over more drinks for them and they turn back to the television. Well, great! Biblical rain, a pompous prick and a cooking course I don't want to do, yippee!

I cast my eye back over the magazine article. There's something about the man in the picture. I don't quite know what it is, the x factor or just good lighting and a talented make-up artist but even so, I rip the article from the magazine and tuck it into my bag. Leaving a tip, I make my way back to my hotel.

Monday

Molly

The hammering rain wakes me from a peculiar dream where wolves howled as I ran barefoot through a forest in a long white, flowing dress. As I come out of the warmth of sleep, it's the screeching wind I can hear, not the sounds of wolves. The wind is coming in through gaps in the windows and making a horrific sound. It's feral and doleful as though there is a warning in the cries, and for some reason it gives me a troubled feeling. I lie in the dark, too awake to sleep but too tired to be awake, listening to the bombardment against the glass before I switch on the bedside lamp. It gives out a weak yellow light before it flickers and goes out. I sigh and throw back the covers, getting up to turn on the overhead light. It's a garish white, or at least the freaky, stormy night makes it appear so, and seems to add to the unnerving feeling that something isn't quite right.

I make a cup of chamomile tea from the selection on the tea tray and drink it standing as close to the window as I can, without being in the cold draft. I was hoping to see the low, full moon but I can barely see the wall of the building opposite, which is only a couple of metres away. The glow of the street lamp at the end of the alley is completely covered by the pouring rain that it's just an orange blur. I don't like it all. Everything feels malevolent and oppressive, and the tapping of the rain onto something hollow below just adds to my unease.

I leave my spot by the window and sit in bed nursing my cup. I just don't want to be here, and I feel horribly unappreciative about that. I've never hated a present before, and it feels alien that I do now, but I've been feeling blue about a lot of things recently, and the weight of negativity is heavy. There seems to be a dark cloud over my head, metaphorically and, looking out the window at the gloom, literally.

For a moment I want to ring Paul, but it's the middle of the night and he's grumpy enough with me during daylight hours, waking him would just give me an earache. Damn it, why am I even here? I fight the urge to throw my cup across the room like a toddler having a tantrum and then I'm distracted by the piece of paper sticking out of my bag. I open the folded sheet and look down on the man, the faded rock star. He's so handsome, breathtakingly so, and his eyes are the reason for the wolves in my dream. I wonder if they're silver in real life, or a trick of the well-placed light. I don't know why I'm so drawn to him, he's not someone I've ever heard of, but there is a pull and a faint whisper. As though in a trance, I trace the outline of his face over and over until I can almost feel the scratches of the stubble on his chin and the rattling outside fades as I stroke the paper.

The next thing I know, my alarm is going off and day has come. Except its bleak, dark grey and the rain is pouring down in sheets.

Wearily I drag myself out of bed and into the meagre shower.

It's going to be a long week.

Jonny

The rain is intense. It clatters against the windows and, from my vantage point in the penthouse, all I can see is a torrent of water that runs from the hill behind the hotel, through the grounds and down to the ocean. There is no distinction between sea and sky, just a vast grey nothing.

I made the mistake of looking at the pictures of Chelsea online and now I feel as shit as the weather. She was the leading story on a showbiz website. Aria was right, she was out in her underwear, her massive fake tits spilling from the tiny lace that didn't do much to keep them in. Her lips were painted the brightest red and the eyelashes she had stuck on, looked like two caterpillars trying to mate. Chelsea resembled the blow-up doll I was given on my eighteenth birthday, and apart from the wedding rings glittering on her hand there was nothing of the woman I married.

She was barely a woman.

They all told me I was making a mistake, but I didn't listen. I was Jonny Raven, and I knew best. I was addicted to Chelsea. She was glorious. Ripe body, insatiable sexual hunger and the perfect mix of slutty and sweet. She charmed everyone but there was no way I was going to let anyone else have her, so I married her. They told me she was too young. She promised I was all she needed, that there would never be anyone else for her so I looked past the big age gap and turned my back on those who said it would never last.

There was such an intensity to our relationship that it consumed us until we couldn't come up for air. We were the golden couple, followed everywhere by a hungry press and Chelsea blossomed under the attention. Then it splintered and we realised there was no common ground to hold us together. The bright golden shine faded to a dull brass, and the intensity faded to an apathy. As my world fell apart, Chelsea got swept up by an in-crowd who gave her the notoriety that I no longer could. Because of me, we lost it all – the money, the houses and the trappings of fame disappeared almost overnight, and our marriage went with it. I wonder what would have happened if I'd listened to those who told me it was all a massive mistake.

The phone rings and I cross the suite to answer it.

"Yes?"

"Mr Raven?" One of the receptionists says, "could you come down please?"

"Is there a problem?"

"No…well, kind of."

"Kind of?"

She stammers, "it's the weather. Mr Cooper is concerned about it affecting the safety of the staff and guests."

"I'm coming." I hang up the phone and throw the cleanest tee-shirt I can find over my head, grimacing as the cuts pull. The suite is a mess. Dirty clothes are strewn over every item of furniture, so I bundle them up and shove them into the washing machine in the kitchenette and throw two washing tablets in after them. There is a flashback to another stinking, filthy hovel and a crying child shivering from the cold and the revulsion twists my gut. Everything I said I would never be, is exactly who I've become.

I strip the greying sheets from the bed and pick damp, musty towels up from the floor, dumping them all beside the washing machine which is making a grinding noise. Hardly surprising, I can't remember the last time I used it. I actually can't really remember the last time I left my

50

suite. I'm self-sufficient up here – a kitchenette with a fridge, cooker and washing machine, a lounge, two bedrooms, a small gym and the bathroom. Not that I have a need for any of it, I've been living in squalor for months, slowly drowning under mountains of festering shit. Fresh produce gets left outside my door, rarely being eaten, just ending up in the bin where it decomposes, the gym gets used when I'm feeling like it, but no one ever comes in. No one really knows I'm here. No one knows I exist anymore. No one apart from a journalist who wanted to stick the knife in further.

I open a window as wide as I dare to hoping some air will clear the foul smell that lingers in the room. The rain plops down onto the window sill, covering a wedding photo so quickly that the colours run, distorting the image. The irony doesn't escape me.

I fill three bin bags of rubbish and carry them down the backstairs. The bins are across from the staff carpark, and I have to run across the flooded tarmac to deposit the bags. The rain is savage, and the water is up to my ankles. I'm completely soaked by the time I get back inside. I take the stairs back up to change then make my way to reception.

The young woman behind the front desk looks up in greeting. Her name badge says Amelia. I don't know when she arrived.

"Is this the only leak?" I ask nodding to a puddle in the doorway.

She looks beyond me to the puddle. "I think it's the only big one, although some of the windows are dripping." I run my finger around the frame of the window closest to me and it comes away wet. Shit.

A cleaner is attempting to clear it up but seems to be fighting a losing battle. I take the mop from him and finish the task quickly. "Can we keep this door closed and use the garden door please?"

"Yes, of course," Amelia says.

"Where's Mr Cooper?"

"He's with a guest in the lounge."

"Do you know what he wanted?"

"Yes, he wanted to ask you about sending everyone home, staff and guests. It means refunding anyone who is staying, or checking in, for the remainder of this week, but the weather is worsening, and the forecast for the next few days is horrific. He's worried that if the sea road gets cut off, which has been reported as inevitable, then no one will be able to leave. The development kitchen is closed, and the restaurant next door isn't opening so Mr Cooper thinks that we should all go too."

Fuck, it's going to be a massive financial hit. "Yes, send everyone home. Do what you need to but do it quickly."

"Shall I arrange a car for you?"

"No, I'll stay."

"Are you sure? If you leave soon, you could join Mrs Raven in London…" Amelia is fishing for a juicy titbit of gossip because a flush spreads across her face.

"As I said, Amelia. I will stay here."

I turn from the room and take the few steps to the bar that leads up into the lounge. Great, here alone, in a storm. I don't think I've ever had a greater burn for whiskey than I do now. Sighing, I walk into the lounge to find the Duty Manager. Why the fuck did I ever buy this hotel?

Molly

"What do you mean by cancelled?" I've just battled my way from the hotel to Chef Patron Brewster's development kitchen in the most petrifying car journey of my life to find the lights off and an out-of-hours phone number taped to the door. The weather is so abominable that the car nearly blew off the road and I almost hit a concrete bollard because the rain made visibility nearly impossible. After all that, the door is locked, and I can just about make out what the miserable woman is at the end of the line is saying. I should have stayed home.

"Cancelled. As in, not happening." I can't really hear her because the sea is thrashing against the beach so angrily it's making my ears ring, but I can tell she doesn't actually care about my predicament.

"Why did no one tell me?" I shout down the line, rubbing futilely at my arms for some warmth.

"Dunno." I'm convinced she shrugged when she said it. "Everyone had a cancellation notice emailed. There is a storm coming…"

"I know! I am standing in it."

"Oh, it'll get worse than this."

"Great, but I didn't get an email…"

"It was sent to the email address on the booking."

"I didn't book it." I say, fighting back tears.

"Then you need to speak to the person who did. I can't help you."

I doubt she could help anyone. I cancel the call not bothering to say 'bye' and stand under the small porch roof expelling a huge growl that erupts, feral and angry, from the pit of my stomach. Then I find Paul's number on my phone and wait for him to answer.

"Oh shit," he says when the call connects. "I meant to ring you. Shit, shit, shit, sorry Molly."

I'm so cross that I can't make my mouth form any words. He *meant* to ring me which means he forgot to ring me even though he knew it was cancelled and now I'm shivering and soaking wet in the worst storm to hit Cornwall in centuries while he is snug and warm at home, probably pretending to work.

"What was more important that you didn't call? Do you have any idea what the weather is like down here? God, Paul, it's awful! I can't see past the end of my bloody nose, and you *meant* to ring…"

"Sorry Moll, I got the email about the course being cancelled last night when I was out on the beers with the lads last night, and then, I over slept and woke up so late for a vlog that I forgot…"

"You forgot?" The silence is long and cold. A stream of water pours off the roof and down the back of my coat forcing me out into the rain.

"It can't be that bad!" He laughs, "you're being a bit overdramatic, Moll, just come on home. You can go back when it's rescheduled."

"Not that bad?" I repeat, snarling at him down the phone. "It is *that* bad Paul. It's freezing, the rain is so thick that I can't see through it, and I can hardly hear you over the waves. I've never seen weather like it and you're telling me it can't be *that bad*. I should never have come. I didn't want to come…" I screw up my face to stop angry tears from falling.

"Moll?"

"I've got to go. There's no one here and it's not safe being this close to the sea. I'm not safe Paul, because you fucking forgot to tell me it was cancelled."

"There is really no need to swear at me, Molly. Drive safely, won't you. I'll take you out to The Bell for dinner."

"Don't fucking bother. I don't want to go anywhere with you."

"Molly…" Paul says in the sing-song patronising voice he often uses when he thinks I'm being silly.

Fuck off, I say under my breath, cancelling the call and shoving my phone into my bag. Then I cry. Noisy, snotty tears that mingle with the rain as I hurry down the path. The sea is ferocious, crashing down with thundering roars onto the beach. Shingle gets thrown upwards and rains down over the break wall, splattering into the surface water like bullets. The spray scratches my face and hands as I try to block as much as I can while I half run, half stagger back to the car.

The sky has turned a sinister murky colour, so dark and malevolent that it's as though the light has been swallowed by a monster. The rain is so thick that I can barely see more than a couple of feet in front of me. I feel dizzy and uncoordinated, and the powerful wind forces me into a twisted, stooped dance from which I fall, over and over, smashing onto my knees and hips until the pain makes me sick. I've been out here for mere moments yet the pace the storm is changing is truly terrifying. The sea is coming closer and closer to the seawall until it eventually breaks over and reaches the road with its long, watery fingers. I should not be here. I should never have come.

The waves slam down onto the road, one after the other, and I stumble on the quaking ground, jarring my aching knees until the wind slams me against the car and the force of it makes me retch, bringing up acidic liquid that I have to spit out. It mixes with the surface water into a phlegmy salty soup and the sight of it floating by my feet, turns my stomach further.

I rummage in my bag for the key fob but I'm so cold that my hands shake violently, and I end up dropping the

55

keyring into the sea water, which is now swirling around the middle of my calves. The panic is breath-taking. I dig in the water, like a dog frantically digging for a bone, screaming each time seaweed wraps itself slimily around my fingers. I can't find them, and the sea just keeps sending waves, each one bigger and stronger than the last, roaring down onto the land then receding back with equal power, taking with them all my hope of finding the keys.

I don't know what to do. I don't know how to save myself. There is nowhere to go where I will be safe from the storm, unless I smash my way into the development kitchen, but I can't see through the sheet of rain to know if that plan would work. Everything feels hopeless. I could drown here, all alone, in a place I didn't want to come, because Paul forgot to tell me. He forgot and I could die because of it. I double up with my arms wrapped around my stomach. Anguish, fear and desperation pools in my gut like a brick and the rain pushes me down into a ball, the wind screaming in my ears and from somewhere inside of the scream there is a voice *it's not your time* and below me, under the grey water is the glint of silver. My keys.

The relief comes out in a whoosh of breath as I reach down for the fob. Somehow, I manage to find the strength to yank the car door open despite the weight of the water and fling myself into the driver's seat. The rain pours in behind me, and the sea water flows in to fill the foot well before I can shut the door. It takes an age to get the keys into the ignition. My fingers are too cold to work properly, and the slamming waves rock the car making my task harder and harder. I pray. To anyone listening. Promising, pleading, beseeching – anything to stay alive. The sobs stick in my throat as I turn the keys begging the car to start, pulling at the steering wheel as though it will help. The car coughs and splutters, stalling over and over as the wet weather gets into the plugs, but eventually it starts, and I wrench it into gear.

I urge the car along the flooded road, moving frighteningly slowly with my foot pushed to the floor in the hope that it will pick up speed, or at least keep going, but the wheels barely move under the water and after a few metres the car dies. I watch in horror as the next wave rears up over the break wall and crashes down onto the bonnet, flipping the car over onto the roof.

The anguished scream is me.

I can't breathe. Water pours in through any gap it can find, and it fills the car until it's a fraction from my nose. It's now, in my final moments, that I understand what true terror is. It's the absence of hope. It's watching a rerun of life in glorious colour, with a sadness that so many opportunities were wasted. I don't want to die. Not like this. Not here, all alone. The terror that has stolen my hope is stealing my breath, with a grip around my neck so tight that I can't get any air into my lungs. I tear at my throat but as I hang upside down, I feel the water rising and the darkness coming for me. I'm going to drown. This is it. The end. I'm going to die before I've ever known true love.

Fight, Molly, fight.

Yes! Yes! I unclip my seatbelt and fall into the water, hitting the roof of the car with my elbow. I have to swallow the sick feeling while I kick my boots against the window. There isn't time for pain as I focus all my attention on smashing the glass. It's hard. The water makes movement slow and difficult, but I keep kicking until enough glass has shattered. I take one breath and swim through the window, the drag of the bag around my neck and soaked clothing making it desperately slow going but managing eventually to find my footing and stand up before the sea turns the car and begins to pull it closer to the break wall. The metal groans against the concrete, a squealing, scratching sound like nails down a chalkboard. The current is strong, but I wade through the water, now up to my waist, as fast as I can manage, away from the monster of the sea.

It takes a lifetime to reach the bank and I scramble as far up it as I can before my exhausted body gives up and I collapse onto the flooded grass. The enormity of the past moments hits me – oh my God, I survived. Against the odds I survived. *You need to move now, Molly. Stand up.* With my last ounce of strength, I pull myself up and turn around to climb up slope. Then I see it.

There is a building, and a light is on.

Jonny

The hotel is empty. The restaurant has been left with breakfast plates on tables and congealing food on the hot plates, but the urgency to get everyone off the peninsula far outweighed the staff clearing up. I sigh and start scraping plates into the bin and pile crockery onto the trolly. I hate the silence. It's just a reminder of how far I've fallen. I clear everything up and take it through to the kitchen, stacking the dishwashers and switching them on. I empty the bins into bags, but the weather has worsened so much that I leave them in the corridor by the back door. There is no way I am going out to the bins, the hotel would be under water the minute I opened the door.

There is a drip coming through the ceiling at the far end of the kitchen, so I stick a bucket under it and walk around the hotel, checking that all the outer doors of the property are secure against the weather. Most of them are solid wood, heavy and unyielding, but there are several with glass panels that need taping up. *How the mighty have fallen* I think as I stand beside the huge reception window and look at the savagery unfolding below. Huge grey waves, foaming with great swaths of white, rise up and crash down onto the road. I can no longer see the sea bridge which is somewhere beyond the sheet of charcoal-coloured rain. It could be the end of the world and I am here completely alone aside from the voices in my head. They are at their most vicious now that there is nothing to take my attention away from them. *Irrelevant. Broke. Faded. Has-be. Wasted. Drunk. Disgusting.* Yeah, yeah, tell me something I don't know.

I do another sweep of the building, taping up any windows that have begun to leak and make my way down the stairs and into the bar.

The bar is my favourite room, not just because it's well-stocked with as much liquor as a man could want, but there is something safe and cocoon-like about its location in the centre of the building with no external windows and doors. Despite the longing for whisky, I pour myself a cola and flop down in a chair to look through Chelsea's social media. It isn't a good thing to do. Chelsea's pages are filled with photos of her almost naked and draped over various leering male celebrities. I stop at a picture of Chelsea kissing the cheek of a footballer, I recognise him as a striker from one of the London clubs. Young, handsome, loaded. He's grinning at the camera while Chelsea's over-plump pout glistens against his skin, her hand on his chest.

She's doing to me what I did to Susie, and Melanie, my wife before her, and all the girlfriends I've had since I was eighteen – I was always looking for the next best thing, like an addiction, women after women, nameless, endless women. Why have one when you can have ten? Why have ten when you can have one hundred... on it went. No regard for anyone's emotions, needs or wellbeing, apart from my own. I lapped up the attention, like a junkie. I took what I wanted and when someone else came along, I went after them and left the one behind without even a backwards glance.

Am I bad person? Most of the time I think I probably am. I feel as though I've gotten everything I deserved and that I lost everything because I wasn't worthy of the talent I'd been given. Maybe if I'd not kept myself so closed off then it wouldn't have happened, but it was always easier to keep everyone at arm's length because I didn't want anyone to know the real me, *the fucking little shit who should never have been born,* so I gave them the celebrity version. Not Chelsea, Susie or Melanie, nor any of the women who ever came into my life would have wanted me if they knew that underneath it all I was quiet and shy, a geek with a crippling lack of confidence. The self-doubt has eaten me up for years, it's why I am now here, in the arse end of nowhere, a forgotten person whose wife would rather be half naked in public than here with me.

Karma is a bitch and she's kicked my arse.

I close Chelsea's page and mindlessly scroll through the lives of musicians I used to know. My peers, my subordinates really, all of whom have stood the test of time, all of whom can still pack out arenas with adoring crowds. Not one of them would have reached my heights back in the day. The good old days. Fuck it. Fuck them. Fuck everything.

My phone beeps once and goes flat. I toss it onto the small coffee table and put my feet up alongside it. I would give anything for one more song. A riff. Even one note would do, it would be start, it would a be a way back but too much time has passed. I can't go back, no matter how badly I want to, because I have no one to take my hand and walk with me, demons and all, into the light.

The silence in the bar is at odds with the hell going on outside. It's unnerving. There is no soft, background music, no chatter, no laughter – nothing but an emptiness that wraps itself around me. I want to blame everyone for where I have ended up, but in the isolation the truth is all too clear. It's my fault. All of it. I let it all go. I got complacent, I didn't listen, thought I knew best, and my arrogance was my undoing. There is no one to blame but me and it's a hard pill to swallow.

I give a resigned sigh and stand up, leaving the bar to search reception for a phone charger. As I cross the tiled floor the lights flicker briefly and go out.

The room is plunged into darkness. For a moment my heart pounds in my chest. "Here's Jonny…" I mutter mirthlessly and cross carefully over to the desk to look for a torch. The front desk is well stocked with everything an emergency situation would need and, I breathe a sigh of relief, there are two large torches and extra batteries. Enough to see me through until the power comes back on, I hope. There isn't a phone charger but as the electricity seems to have gone off completely, it wouldn't matter if there had been one. Then I stand up sharply. Fuck! Someone is hammering on the door.

I cross the room quickly and unlock the door, bracing myself against the force of the wind and rain that come pounding in as I open it. "Oh my God!" I say aghast as a small figure collapses onto me. They are soaked through to the skin and icy cold, shivering so violently that I stagger backwards, my arm tightening around their slim frame. We both jump as the door slams against the inside wall, knocking down a picture that shatters onto a table. It takes seconds for the reception floor to disappear under an ankle-deep flood of rainwater. Through the shudders and sobs I can hear *car, sea, drown, help* in a desperate female voice.

"Has someone drowned?" I ask horrified, my heart picking up the pace and crashing against my ribs. "Does someone need help?"

I think she shakes her head against my chest but she's shuddering so much that I can't tell.

"Are you sure? Are you alone?" She raises terrified eyes up at me. Streaks of mascara have run down her pale face and her short hair is stuck up with clumps of seaweed and grass. She nods once and looks beyond me to the sea. I follow her gaze. Shit, the sea has begun to creep its way up the hill towards us. "I need to let you go for a moment," I can feel her heart racing through her sodden clothing, and the slenderness of her frame as she grips me tighter. "It's ok, you'll be ok, but I need to bolt the door."

She takes her hands from around me and leans against the wall as I fight to close the door. The rain is sharp and the effort to close the door pulls against the cuts on my torso. I'm sure they're bleeding again. I turn the key and slam the bolts across. "Who are you? I didn't think there was anyone left this side of town."

She mumbles, "Molly. I'm Molly," then she turns a sickly colour of yellow, slumps forward and crashes down into the water.

Shit. Shit. Shit. I reach for Molly, pulling her up out of the water and shift her so she's facing me, but her head is lolling backwards, and her eyes are closed. Lying my fingers across the pulse point on her neck I check for a heartbeat. There is one, it's slow but it's there, thank fuck. I heave her into a fireman's lift and carry her to the bar, lying her down on the sofa. Molly's skin is a deathly pale grey, even in the darkness, and she's so still, the shivering has stopped and there is a quiet about her that fills me with panic.

"That can't be good," I say to no one. What do I do? She could be dying for all I know. Fuck. What do I do? I run up the stairs, tripping over myself in my haste to the first bedroom I come to and realise I've left the key behind the front desk. Fuck, fuck, fuck. My feet barely hit the floor until I slip on the bottom step and jarring my ankle which sends excruciating pain around my body. I don't wait for the nausea to subside, instead I grab the key and rush back upstairs, ignoring the protests of my ankle and take the duvet off the bed, taking the stairs down two at a time.

I've wasted precious time, but she is still breathing, it's shallow and barely audible but it will do. I yank the wet clothes from her body, leaving her underwear in place, and roll her up in the duvet. Then I sit, wait and pray. I fucking pray. And I wait. And I pray. The clock ticks and I still wait.

***

I don't like the silence. My mind is strangely quiet, and the absence of the inner voices has made me realise just how much I've depended on the daily onslaught for company. Sitting in the bar, with the wind howling through reception and a stranger on the sofa in her underwear, is not how I thought today would go. I haven't dared leave the room in case she succumbs to hyperthermia, although the pink spots that have appeared on her cheeks since she was wrapped in the duvet means I can breathe a little easier. A small sigh escapes her lips and I take it as a sign that I can at least do another quick check of the building.

The front door is still holding and aside from taping up some extra windows, the hotel seems to be withstanding the storm. I look in on the woman and begin mopping up the water from the floor of reception. It doesn't take long but with the cuts still pulling, it's hard going. I leave the mop and bucket in front of the desk and walk up the steps back to the bar.

She is awake.

"Hi." I say, sitting down opposite her. "How are you feeling?"

"Like I've lost a fight with the Kraken." Molly manages a small smile.

"I bet! You looked like it too when you came crashing through the door!" I grin at her, "why were you even out in it? We've had weather warnings for days."

"I know!" She shudders and her voice breaks. "I was meant to be doing a course with Chef Patron Brewster,

64

but it got cancelled and no one told me." She starts crying, great, big sobs that have her bent over as she tries to control herself. "The waves came over my car and the engine stopped. I thought I was going to die...so much water...the car...I don't know how I got out." She's shivering so hard that her teeth rattle. "Then I saw your light." She smiles weakly and takes some big, deep breaths. "But it went out as I was climbing up the bank and it's so dark outside that I couldn't really see where I was going. I fell over a lot..." Her voice breaks. "I have no clothes, nothing...Everything I have is in a hotel in town or in my car." Her face crumples again and fat tears roll onto her cheeks.

"Don't cry, it will all be ok. You're safe here, this building has survived more than one mega storm in its time, it will survive this one." The whistling coming from the reception seems to say, *are you sure about that* but I close my ears to the thought that we will be anything other than safe. "I can offer you a room, a hot bath at least while the gas is still working, and if you don't have anything, I can also give you some clothes, they'll be mine, and massive on you, but better than nothing."

"Thank you." She hesitates and worry flickers in her bloodshot eyes as she looks beyond me to the pile of wet clothes. "Why are my clothes on the floor?"

"I took them off you..."

"You took them off?" Molly's face floods with crimson, "oh my God."

"I didn't look! I promise. I just wanted to keep you alive and get you warm quickly. Survival one-oh-one!"

"Oh my God," she repeats, wrapping her arms over the duvet and holding it tight against her. "I mean, thanks for saving my life, but...I'm literally in my worst underwear."

I laugh. "I promise I didn't look!"

I hear her mumble something and worry crosses her face.

"You are safe here, Molly. I'm not a psycho or a serial killer and I've never kidnapped anyone! I own this hotel but if it will make you feel better, there is a baseball bat in the games room I can get for you if you want to use it at any point!"

"I didn't think…"

"Honestly, I would have thought all sorts if I'd woken up in a strange place, in a blackout, in my pants with a stranger telling me I was ok, so I get why you feel the way you do." I smile at Molly. "You really are safe, I'm perfectly normal." *That's the biggest lie of all.* "Can I get you a drink? Water? Something stronger?"

"Water would be good please. My throat feels full of salt." She says and I cross the room to the bar to fill a glass from the water pump. Molly wriggles up to sitting taking care to keep the duvet wrapped around her. "So, who are you?"

"I'm Jonny." I walk back to her and hand her the glass.

"Nice to meet you Jonny," then she stops. "Oh." She says, surprise filling her face.

"Oh?"

"Oh, it's you."

Molly

"Who's me?" Jonny shifts and the atmosphere suddenly becomes heavy and tense.

"Sorry, you just look like someone…never mind." My throat is sore from the screaming and the dryness of my mouth makes my words more clipped. I feel awkward. He may not be looking at me, but I know he's the person in the magazine. The strange silver eyes are far too unusual for this to be a coincidence. I drink the water down in one go but my salt-water-filled stomach isn't happy and tries to send it back up. My hand flies to my mouth. *Don't be sick, Molly, don't be sick.* "Urgh," I groan.

"Are you alright?"

"Imgonnabesick…"

My body starts shaking and acid forms in my mouth. Oh God, not only am I in my worst pants and a bra that's seen better days, but it's likely I will vomit all over my host's carpet. *Breathe, Molly, breathe.* I take deep breaths but there is no stopping the rising up of my stomach contents. Jonny puts the bar bin down just in time.

"Ohmigodimsorry." I hurl the words into the bin. Tears spring to my eyes as I cough and retch and vomit until there is nothing left in my stomach. Jonny rubs my back with soft and warm hands. *Oh hell, Molly, of all the times to notice that.* Then I become painfully aware that my left boob has left the safety of my bra and is dangling free. I don't know how I'm going to get it back into the cup without letting go of the bin. What a mess, what an absolutely stinking, crusty, almost-died mess and then I really cry.

The sobs rock my body, but I manage to put my breast away before Jonny notices. It's bad enough that I'm bawling like a crazy person, but he doesn't need to see that nothing remains of my dignity.

I'm pretty sure I'll end up with some long-lasting trauma from the terrifying situation I've found myself in. My stomach twists with a strange grief that I've become so unimportant to Paul that I didn't leave Cornwall when it was safe to. I squeeze my eyes tightly shut to stop the tears from falling but they fall anyway, and I feel completely exposed in my near naked, sobbing state. I don't think I can ever look Jonny in the eye again. Even if they are bewitching wolf eyes that I can feel on me as I hurl one more time into the bin.

I am literally living in a nightmare.

"I'm so embarrassed," I mutter from inside the bin. My vomit is a stomach-churning mix of coffee and salt water, but I can't make my head move because there is safety inside the bin, even if it's the worst smelling sanctuary possible.

"Please don't be."

"Easy for you to say, I didn't undress you..."

Shut up Molly, shut up.

I can't smell the contents of the bin any longer so I slowly - really, really slowly - lift my head up and look straight at Jonny. Damnit. It was not my intention to catch his eye, and clearly, I'm not endearing myself to him because he is now staring at me like I've got two heads. After the events of this morning, anything is possible – two heads, green scales, a tail - who knows what I look like.

"Shall I show you to a room?" He asks.

"Yes please." It comes out like a sigh of relief. It is a sigh of relief. It's a *yay I can claw back some dignity*, and Jonny must feel equally relieved as he gestures for me to follow him. He picks up my sopping bag from on top of the pile of clothes, and the torch that was on the table and we walk in silence, me with the duvet wrapped as tightly around me as is possible, up three flights of stairs to a room at the top of the hotel.

Jonny unlocks the door of a huge, square room in a corner of the building. There is a balcony that would, I presume, overlook the ocean but there is nothing to see apart from the thick grey rain.

"Is this ok for you?" He asks putting my handbag down on the floor and flashing the light around the room. "It's the largest suite I have. There is a mini bar, so please help yourself to whatever you like, although the kettle won't work with the power outage, but there are plenty of soft drinks and you can stock up with anything else from the cellar. I'll show you where that is later. There are toiletries in the bathroom and more in the housekeeping cupboard if you run out. The gas still works so there is lots of hot water, especially now the hotel is empty."

"Thanks, the room is great." Nothing is great, I'm half naked and relying on the kindness of a complete stranger. It's all sucky. So bloody sucky. I pull the duvet tighter around me and burst into tears again. "Sorry, I don't mean to cry, you're being so nice..." I don't have a spare hand to wipe the tears away, so Jonny pick up a box of tissues from the rectangular coffee table and uses one to wipe my face. He's gentle, too gentle and it just makes me cry more. "My car is probably half way to France..." The wailing that follows is way too melodramatic, but I can't help it. It's a shitty, shitty day and I feel desolate.

Jonny doesn't say anything just squishes me and the duvet into a big hug. His arms don't really wrap around me, but the sentiment is nice, and he smells really good, citrusy and musky with a tinge of sea water, probably from my arrival, and I lean into him, resting the tip of my forehead onto his firm chest. "You're safe here Molly, I promise. All storms pass eventually, even this one."

"Ok." I whimper. *Oh, come on Molly, stop being so wet. You're alive. Just stand there for a moment and breathe – but not too deeply, he smells too good. Molly! What? Stop it!*

"Why don't you run a bath and I'll get you some dry clothes?"

I smile. "Thank you for being my knight in shining armour. If you'd not been here to open the door, well, I don't want to consider what would have happened to me."

Jonny grins and does an embellished bow. "You're welcome fair maiden! Take as long as you like then come downstairs when you're ready and I'll make some food, although I should warn you that I'm not the greatest cook!"

"Thanks."

Jonny nods and walks across the suite, closing the door behind him. I take a massive breath in. Then I burst into tears again. The sobs are noisy, snotty and dribbly and I half stagger, half collapse onto the small sofa, clutching my stomach as though to hold myself together. I feel slimy and filmy and so, so cold but I can't make myself move. Every single ounce of energy has left me, and this morning already feels like I've lived a lifetime. I'm desperately tired but there's no chance of sleep because each time I close my eyes I see the wave coming for me.

When the sobs finally stop, I drag myself up from the sofa. It's an effort. Everything hurts now that the adrenaline has worn off and I am certain I've aged five decades. I pick up the torch and walk stiffly to the bathroom, carrying my sodden bag that leaves a trail of droplets on the carpet.

I push open the door and walk to the bath. I put the plug in and turn the hot tap onto full, pouring liberal amounts of expensive bubble bath under the faucet. I strip off my crusty underwear and catch sight of myself in the mirror. Holy hell, what a mess. Makeup is streaked down my face, and I have seaweed in my hair. My body is covered in bruises, and I have cuts on my legs from kicking out the window of the car. I look horrific.

When the bath is full, I sink into the hot, scented bubbles. Yawn after yawn stretch my jaw and although it feels like I've been awake forever, it's only been about four hours. Four hours in which I escaped death and crashed into the life of someone who used to be famous once. It doesn't seem real. Perhaps I'll wake up soon and I'll be safe at home, working hard on my business, happy with Paul and never being any the wiser about a man with hypnotic eyes and a perfect bottom living in Cornwall. Because he does have a perfect bottom, I accidentally noticed once or twice.

I jump when my phone begins to ring shrilly from inside my soaking bag. I'd forgotten all about my phone thinking it had been lost with the car. I drag myself up to lean over the bath, reaching as far as my arm will stretch to get it from the pocket of the bag.

It's Paul. I sigh and feel so unsure about answering it, that I hesitate long enough for the call to go to voicemail. I don't want to speak to him because right now I don't see a future for us. For months now I thought everything was my fault, that I sacrificed our relationship when my new career took off. My former job as a forensic accountant didn't fill me with the joy that my interiors business does now, but life was so much easier then - good money, good life, good relationship – but 'Polly' got lost when I found my passion. *Can you still not see that 'Polly' got lost when things were no longer on Paul's terms?*

I chuck my phone on the floor and slide under the water. I don't want to think about Paul, he can wait.

71

Jonny

It's gotten darker if that was even possible. There is no longer anything to see outside just an expanse of dark grey nothing. I wander around the hotel with the torch, checking the windows and doors remain secure. Most are, but I'm not convinced the conservatory will survive. It was already buckling under the pounding from the elements and that was before the storm worsened. I don't want to consider the cost of replacing it, but that's a worry for another day. *Why the fuck did you buy this shit pile,* I crossly ask myself for the millionth time.

I don't blame Chelsea for never wanting to come here, I wish I could just up and leave, but there is nowhere else to go, and my wife has made it clear that she doesn't want me with her. My friends dropped me when my career ended up down the fucking toilet and Fred proved that our relationship was based on what I could pay him, so that's it. There is no one left. It feels fucking heart-breaking. It also feels like my entire life has been a lie, just smoke and mirrors. Aria is the only person who still fights my corner, but even she tries not to come here.

There should be a place that failed musicians can go to find solace, find their voice again, whatever they need just not be in an isolated hell with only memories for company. I wish Chelsea was the kind of wife that would support me and help get me back up on a stage again, but she will never, ever be that person. It's too much effort. I'm too much effort. I wonder what she is doing while I'm here with only a complete stranger for company, but there is a freedom to having a flat phone and no electricity – it is saving my fragile self from any more photographic evidence that my wife is after the next wealthy man.

I should just divorce her.

I'm an idiot for hanging on.

It has to be worse to be lonely in a relationship than lonely alone. *Do you love Chelsea?* Well, that's the million-pound question. *Did you ever?*

The melancholy thoughts tighten their grip and the familiar narrative spins around my head telling me I'm the reason I have nothing. I wish it was because I made the wrong choices, trusted the wrong people but the truth is, it was all me. Desperate for approval, desperate to be someone, desperate to escape a shitty past – all I did was swap one wank life for another, one sense of emptiness for an emptiness that feels even worse.

I check the final windows on the top floor of the hotel and pause for a moment outside of Molly's room. She seems sweet, and remarkably sane for someone who nearly drowned. I consider knocking on the door to check on her, but figure she probably wants to have some time to process the morning, so instead I take the stairs back down and flop in a chair across from the reception desk. It doesn't matter what I don't have, I have Aria, and she is enough. *Keep telling yourself that, Jonny.* I get lost in my thoughts until Molly speaks to me from the top of the stairs.

"Hi! Thank you for the clothes." Molly gestures to her body with the torch. The joggers have been rolled up, so the cuff is thick around her ankle, and pulled in so tight at the waist that the hips bag. The old band tee-shirt swamps her small frame. "Am I rocking the look?" She grins shyly.

I flick my torch up. "You're looking much better than when you first arrived!"

Molly laughs. "I'm not sure I could ever look worse than that. Is it ok if I join you?"

"Absolutely. Did you have everything you needed?"

"I sure did. There's so much stuff in the room, I'm surprised your guests don't stay permanently. If I had all those toiletries, I'd never leave the bathroom!"

"You'd be surprised…" I mutter.

"Then they are fools!" Molly says smiling, "I feel completely spoilt! I wanted to top up the hot water and stay in the bath all day, then I thought, oh my God, what if the gas goes off and I used all the hot water up and we end up stinking…"

"Do you often think this much?" I ask her lightly.

"No, not usually, but then it's not every day that I face a life-and-death situation!" Her stomach makes an almighty rumble.

"Come on, Molly, let's raid the kitchen. Chef had a huge delivery yesterday so even if the gas goes off and we sit around stinking, we'll at least be well fed."

"That's good in theory…"

"But?" I ask.

"But how will we cook feasts without gas?"

"Damnit, you've got me on that one!"

There is a long pause as our eyes lock and two spots of pink cover the cheeks of Molly's pale face. She is really pretty, cute actually, in a natural, girl-next-door kind of way. Nothing is inflated or lifted, and the softness of her body under the too-big clothing seems so normal after Chelsea's gym-obsessed, surgically enhanced figure. I shouldn't compare them, but it's hard not to, and I hate myself for it.

Molly jumps as the wind forces a window open and the rain comes streaming in banging the window against the wall. The bang is dulled only slightly by the thick crimson curtain. "Holy shit." She says, going white. I force the window shut and she darts across the room to lean against it as I coerce the latch into place. "When is this storm going to end?"

"We have a few more days of this," I tell her. "It's going to get worse before it gets better."

"Great." She groans and two fat tears roll down her cheeks. She doesn't wipe them away.

She doesn't want to be here.

No one wants to be here.

Molly

He looks upset. He tries to mask it, but he has misconstrued my words and I think explaining would just make things worse. I sneak a glance at him as he gives his full attention to the window. Jonny looks like his photo, just older and more tired, but his eyes are haunted and there is a sallow-ness to his skin, as though he is grieving for something. I have the strangest longing to reach out, take his hand and tell him everything will be ok, but he's now checking the fastenings and even if he wasn't, it would be weird if I did. I have no idea if everything will be ok.

I wipe my eyes and smile, "sorry, that came out wrong. I don't like the storm…"

"I'm not surprised." He finishes his task, wipes his hands on his jeans and walks across the room. "I need to find a couple of extra torches or candles, and then we'll get some food." He rummages in a cupboard behind the reception desk, banging his head on a shelf as he does, before pulling out a bunch of candles. "God knows where they keep the matches," Jonny says rubbing his head, "there's none in here. I wonder if there is any in the bar."

I take a big breath in. "Do you have any brandy in your bar? I can't seem to stop my hands from shaking and it might just take the edge off." I usually hate brandy, but I'm a sucker for the movies and that's what everyone seems to drink when the world is about to end.

"Brandy I can definitely do. Come with me but watch your step because the floors aren't flat."

I follow him to a room beyond the foyer, tripping up a few small steps that I don't see. "I always wondered what it would be like to live in a hotel with everything on tap." I offer as conversation.

"It's lonely. Great food, but lonely."

"No wife?" I ask, then I wish I hadn't. Jonny freezes momentarily but it's enough for me to realise the probable reason for the sadness that emanates from him.

"Sometimes. When she wants something. Money, mainly." He says with a sigh. "She hates Cornwall. London has the bright lights so that's where she wants to be, and she resents me for moving us here."

"Oh." Well, she sounds like an ungrateful bitch. Although listening to the storm screaming outside, I don't blame her for wanting to be in London. I don't know what to say and the word just hangs in the air. Jonny finds some matches on the mantle and lights the candles, casting a warm glow over the room. "That's better," I say, switching off my torch and sitting down in a chair beside the wood burner. "When did the lights go out?"

"Not long before you banged on my door."

"I bet it was creepy being here in the dark." I muse. "In such an old building with ghosts and stuff." Somewhere something bangs and we jump.

"I didn't think about the ghosts!" Jonny smiles, adding wood to the burner. "But it wasn't much fun being here alone in the dark."

I like how he speaks, a subtle northern twang, inflections on certain words, and the deep voice. He takes a candle and walks behind the bar, setting two glasses on the polished wood and pouring large measures into them from a bottle on the back. "I've gone generous!" He laughs, "I'm supposed to be giving up drinking, but this is an emergency situation." I watch him carry the glasses back with two bags of peanuts held between his teeth and he sits down opposite me.

"Why?" I ask, taking the peanuts from him and putting them onto the table. He puts the glasses down and sits opposite me, resting his feet on the spare chair.

"Because it's been too much of a comfort recently." He pauses, "actually, a lot longer than I would like to admit."

His honestly feels raw, as though it's the first time he's said it out loud.

"Are you an alcoholic?" I ask.

"No, but there has been a dependency on it that I'm ashamed of."

"We all have our things," I say. "My comfort is chocolate. I lost my job eighteen months ago and I literally ate massive slabs of it every single day. I even went out specifically for it, no necessities, just chocolate. I gained a stone, got spots…I was disgusting. It's different now but I think everyone has something they lean on when things get tough. We look for something to warm us, or save us…everyone does it, the trouble is we beat ourselves up for what that thing does to us. For me it was getting chubby and spotty, it would have been a different outcome for you and for the next person."

"Excess has been part of my life," he says, nursing his glass. "It came with the job and then everything got so bleak…"

I wonder if I should tell him I read the article, but he stares into space and I don't want to interrupt his thoughts. I rip open one of the peanut bags and crunch them between my teeth until I'm conscious of the noise I'm making. I put the bag down and pick up the glass. The brandy doesn't taste as bad as I thought it would.

"I think excess is part of life generally," I say when he finally moves. "We all chase more and more and more, nothing is enough."

"Maybe." He replies, taking a long sip of the brandy. I watch him, without meaning to. Jonny doesn't seem to notice as I gaze at his strong profile, the straight nose, long eye lashes, full lips and rugged jaw. I look until he catches my eye and then I feel embarrassed for staring. He's probably used to it though, if the article was true. "Right then, Molly," he says, "a woman cannot survive on brandy and peanuts alone, I'll make you some proper food."

"Good man!" I say, draining my glass. Jonny finishes his then takes me through the hotel. It's hard to make it out by torchlight but it's a lot bigger than I'd imagined. There are corridors leading off corridors, until eventually we get to the kitchen.

I wave my torch around the room. Even in the dim light the kitchen looks immaculate. "I've never been in a kitchen that is this tidy! Mine never ever looks like this!" I lean against a stainless-steel counter. "You know you've made it in life if you have a kitchen like this!"

"Or you've failed in life," he mutters. "It wouldn't look like this, if it was left to me," Jonny laughs and it takes the edge off his words, "I'm the messiest person I know."

"I bet I could beat you on that!"

Jonny rummages in the fridge. "What do you fancy?" He asks, his voice muffled.

"What do you have?"

"It's more a question of what I can cook."

I giggle. "That's my kind of menu! What will go out of date first?"

"Steak?"

"For lunch? That is posh!" I set my torch down and direct the beam so it lights as much of the room as possible. "I got stranded in the right place!"

Jonny pulls steaks out of one fridge and salad from another. "I'm glad you got stranded here," he says quietly.

"I'm glad too." I reply, and it's true, I am glad. Jonny feels safe, in a strange way. In real life I would be unnerved about it, but post-trauma I feel wrapped up by the old building and the sad soul I am with. He's not said much but the aura that surrounds him is melancholy. I want to ask him about the article, but it doesn't seem like the right time. I'm not sure there will ever be a right time. How to you ask a person if they are the has-been that a journalist claims they are? It's not the sort of thing you mention over steak.

"Ooh," I say, "you have a radio in here! Can I put it on? Oh," I feel my face fall. "There's no power."

"It's battery operated," Jonny replies. "We often have power cuts here and Chef hates not having music in the kitchen."

"I'm the same! I always have music on when I'm working, it helps me think. Paul hates it…"

"Who's Paul?" Jonny asks. I feel my body tense up and my jaw tighten. It's a surprising reaction.

"My boyfriend…" A flicker of anger begins to burn in my stomach and I unexpectedly want to add *for now* to the statement.

"Why does he hate it?"

"We have completely different tastes in music. He likes arty farty stuff that sounds all new age-y and I like pop. Loud pop. Pop that I can sing along to at top of my voice! I can't sing in tune at all, but it's never stopped me from belting out a song! I'm a total karaoke queen! It was fine when I went out to work because I just sang in the car on the commute and he didn't have to listen to it, but we both work at home now, so he just complains all the time."

"What does he do?"

"He's a sports vlogger. It's very popular and he does well from it, but he particularly loves it when he gets spotted by sports fans and is asked for a selfie, like he's a famous person. He's always wanted to be famous and now milks it. It's pretty embarrassing really."

"You didn't like the fame stuff then?"

"No." I shake my head, "because it isn't fame really. I mean, his channel does really well, well enough for him to do it full time, and he works hard but when we're out and he's accosted by avid football fans it just annoys me. I'd understand it if he was a player, but..." I chew my lip. "The trouble is that he likes being *someone*, and being the only *someone* in our house, so then he just got resentful of me because I gained a social media following that turned into a new business." I shrug, "None of it has done us any favours as a couple. Our successes are not good for our relationship." I pause. "Well, my success hasn't been..."

"Lack of success isn't good for relationships either." Jonny tells me.

"Shit, isn't it?"

"Yep," he says with a big sigh. "Do you need to phone home? Paul would probably want to know you're safe, although I don't know if the phones are working, I've not actually checked. You can try if you want to?"

"My phone still works but no, I don't. I don't want to speak to him. I need a break, or something..." Then I burst into noisy, shuddering tears. Jonny leans over and hug me. He feels so strong and comfortable that I stand against him for longer than I should. Shit. He smells really good and without meaning to, I nestle into the firmness of his chest. It's hard against my cheek, but it makes me feel safe, and he just lets me cry. I'm not sure why I'm crying, I don't feel sad, just angry and unhappy. So unhappy. How long have I been unhappy for? Paul stopped paying attention to me when my business took off. It happened so fast. I went from a couple of Instagram posts to a website and a flourishing business within months. He hates it. Resents it. Doesn't listen

82

when I talk about work. As long as I pay my share of the bills, he has no interest in what I do. I think he is jealous because he loved being the only one who was well-known. He hates the international recognition and interest I've gained. I have what he wants. It's why he bought me a present he knew I wouldn't like, and why he didn't tell me it was all cancelled. Suddenly everything makes sense.

I stop crying with a huge shuddering breath that makes my brain rattle. "Sorry." I mumble, "you must think I'm a total idiot!"

Jonny laughs. I like his laugh, it's melodic and light. "I don't think anything of the sort."

I dry my eyes on the tee-shirt I'm wearing. "Phew!"

"You never know, Molly, we may end up having a great day, stranger things have happened! The kitchen is full, and the gas is on! We even have board games somewhere…"

"Oooh, I love board games although I should warn you that I'm very competitive!"

"The challenge is set, my friend, prepare to lose!"

"Ha, you wish!"

***

Jonny is a much better cook that he gave himself credit for. The steak cuts like butter and the salad I rustle up from all the goodies in the fridges is a great accompaniment. "We are a catering dream team!" I say, feeling much cheerier than I did five hours earlier.

The storm is still raging outside and the wind whistles around the building like a malevolent ghost, but I feel safe. It's comfortable here. We're in the small bar in the centre of the building with lit candles on every surface.

Jonny was concerned that the torches would use the batteries too quickly and the hotel has such a mammoth stock of candles that we opted for that. The light is soft and makes the room feel cosy. I can't remember the last time I felt so relaxed, which surprises me. I nearly died today, my relationship may have ended today and I'm in a strange man's underwear, but there is a calmness here that is unexpected despite those things.

Jonny grins, "we sure are." He tops up my wine glass with the expensive red wine he'd chosen. "Don't worry," he says as my eyebrow rises by itself, "this is sociable and not a reflection of my 'thing'.

"Sorry about my judgemental eyebrow," I reply smiling, "the rest of me isn't judging you at all because the gooey chocolate pudding I saw in the dessert fridge is calling my name and I've already told you about my relationship with chocolate!" I lean back in the chair. "I think I like this room the best, not being able to hear the storm almost makes it not there."

"I like this room the best too," Jonny says, "and when I thought I was going to have to ride the storm out alone, I contemplated moving in here. Not for the drink…" He adds quickly, "you being here has probably saved me from my demons."

"I think it may be saving me from mine too."

Jonny doesn't ask me what I mean, and I'm glad of that. I wouldn't know what to say, even if he had. How would I explain to a stranger that there is a relief to be away from Paul's constant moans and criticisms, that it feels as though a huge weight has lifted. I always thought Paul and I were destined for forever, but the past eighteen months, or so, has just proven than he doesn't have my back and I'm not sure I have his. We don't talk, we don't go to bed together, often I'm in the spare room due to working late, and the shared interests have fallen away.

Everything we do now is separate. When we go out for dinner there is a silence that is awkward and heavy and centres around 'are you enjoying your meal?' or 'would you like another drink?' Paul liked being the famous one, he doesn't like that my business has put me on the map.

Jonny stands up and picks up the stack of plates, "let's get dessert, lots of dessert! It all has to be eaten before it goes off, so we'll be doing Chef a favour!"

"Are you worried about losing all that money?" I ask, following him to the kitchen. "Full fridges and no residents?"

"When you have no money, you can't worry about having less."

Jonny's admission surprises me, and the surprise must show on my face because he says, "did you assume I had lots?"

"I read an article about you." I admit, feeling certain it was the right time to confess to knowing who he is. "In a magazine. I recognised your eyes and I'd assumed…"

The plates smash onto the floor.

Jonny

I didn't mean to drop the plates. I didn't plan on doing anything other than serving up big slabs of dessert, but she caught me off guard. Molly's looking in horror at the broken crockery, her face an ashen white, and is probably wishing she could take the words back, because that's my wish too. I wish she could have made up her own mind about me, not base everything on the opinions of some journalist who I've probably never met. So, what does she think of me now? That I'm a fuck up? A sad, lonely, talentless, fuck up. That I had it all and lost it because I'm a fucking idiot? It makes a mockery of the past few hours. She had already made up her mind.

"Should I not have told you?" Molly asks, her face crumpling. She is chewing and pulling on her lip as though she has absolutely no idea what to do next. "I didn't want to not tell you, because that would be weird, because I'm staying here. It would have been worse if I mentioned I'd read about you tomorrow or the next day. Wouldn't it? Shit. Shit." She crouches down and starts collecting the broken crockery into a pile. Her back rises and falls rapidly, almost as though she can't catch her breath. "I didn't think anything bad of you," she whispers. "I didn't judge you on what I read. No one has it easy all the time, regardless of the hand they're dealt..." Her voice breaks.

"It's ok, Molly." I say kneeling down beside her to help pick up the pieces of porcelain. "I've been incognito for years, it was just a bit of a shock to have been recognised."

"Sorry about your plates."

"They were inherited with the hotel, don't worry about it."

"For what it's worth, I thought the journalist was an arse."

"They usually are."

She puts the pieces into a pile. "What was it like to be famous? I can't really imagine it."

"Amazing, scary, claustrophobic and it spoilt me rotten. I wasn't a nice person back then. You wouldn't have wanted to have been washed up with that version of me!"

"Oh? Why?" She asks, curiosity on her face.

"Because I would have taken you to bed and binned you off the next day!"

Molly flushes. "Charming! I may not have wanted to go to bed with you!"

"You would have, they all did." I say it matter-of-factly, without boasting. It was true, every woman wanted to sleep with me back then - groupies, housewives, socialites – no one ever said no, not like now.

"I'm not *all women* though, Jonny."

I study her face and she stares back at me with clear eyes. "No, you're not." I smile. "You are a breath of fresh air, but if I were a betting man, I'd put money on you succumbing to my charms once upon a time." I laugh and the two spots of pink return to her cheeks. It's nice that I can make her blush even though her gentle ways would have been trampled on in the good old days, whatever she says. I'm glad Molly got washed up at my door, being with her feels comfortable, and she is so pretty that I could look at her all day. Which isn't a good thing because it means that Jonny Raven may not be completely dead and buried after all. I push those thoughts away and say, "leave the mess Molly, that chocolate pudding won't eat itself!"

✳✳✳

"Is it true what that journalist wrote about you?" Molly asks, taking a spoonful of pudding, "or was it creative license?"

"Mostly true," I admit, pouring more cream into my bowl. "The record sales, the concerts and the excesses, pretty much all of it was accurate." I hadn't wanted to read the article, but I did. It was pandora's box that called and called me from the coffee table until I gave in and read it. Now I wish I hadn't.

"What happened?" Molly raises the spoon to her mouth, and I watch as her naturally plump lips open. *For fucks sake, Jonny, stop it.*

"I was around eighteen when I got my record deal, and it was a hard slog for a couple of years until one day my image and my music was literally everywhere. I couldn't even go to the corner shop for a pint of milk without crowds forming outside. Eventually I had to get security and then house staff to do all that for me. Then came the excess which piled on top of excess – I had everything I'd ever wanted! Fame, glory, money, talent, women! Property in all the best locations - a loft in New York, a beach fronted condo in Malibu, a chic apartment in SoHo, a top floor penthouse in Monaco – it was all mine and I finally felt like I'd made it."

"I can imagine," Molly says licking her spoon clean of chocolate sauce. "But how much is too much? I can't imagine having so much money that I could buy all those houses. It's a whole different world to the one I know!"

"Despite what most people believe, there is only so much money a person can spend, particularly if you're earning what I did. Unless you want to build a rocket that will go into space, things like that will swallow hefty sums, but for the average person, once you've got the cars, the watches, the women, the designer labels, the

88

speedboats and the property, there isn't really anything else to buy. It's when the money stops coming, and the spending continues you then have a problem."

"Is that what happened to you?"

"Yes. I lost it all almost overnight, or it felt like it! This hotel is all I have left, and I hate it. It's not a home, that's for sure."

"Why did you keep it and not one of the other houses?"

"Because it pays for itself. I didn't have the money to keep any of the others."

Molly falls silent and I can see questions flashing over her face. Eventually she says, "I think as humans we just have two basic needs – somewhere to live and people to love. I'm not sure it does us any favours to have too much, not really."

"I totally agree with you, coming from a place of having had too much. I've got somewhere to live, so better off than some, and I have Aria. I don't suppose it really matters that I've not ever had the sort of love that doesn't come with a price tag, well apart from her."

"Who's Aria?"

"My daughter. She's amazing. Nothing fazes her at all. She doesn't have any hang ups, which blows my mind, particularly as she has me for a father! She wants to be an archaeologist, but she could be a singer if she wanted. She has a pitch perfect voice and is level headed enough to avoid all the pitfalls. I'm so proud of her, she's the best thing I've ever achieved."

"Given everything you have achieved, she must be incredible."

I smile, "she really is."

"Then what happened? How did you not find love when you were…well…you?" Molly asks. "I would have thought love would have come easily when you're at the top of the pecking order."

"It was never real because it all came at a price, and the price was fame and notoriety."

"Sounds lonely."

"It was. I didn't realise that while I was living it, but the last five years..." I stop talking. I don't want to tell Molly about Chelsea. I don't want her to ask why I'm still married to someone who can't be in the same room as me for longer than an hour. I don't want Molly to know how pathetic I am. "Karma." I say eventually, "karma made me pay for it all. Would you like any more pudding?"

I wonder if she notices that I change the subject, but she shakes her head and replies, "no thanks, I'm well and truly full!" Molly doesn't ask any more questions and I'm glad of that. She's too easy to talk to and I already feel as though I've said more than I should have. My past isn't endearing, and I pushed it too much when I said I would have taken her to bed. *Damnit, Jonny.* "I'm not too full to whoop your arse at games though," she says grinning, "I was the snakes and ladders champion at primary school."

"The challenge is set, prepare to lose!"

"You wish, Jonny, you wish!"

Molly

I make coffee by boiling a saucepan of water and we sit drinking it around a small table in the bar. In front of us, Jonny has set up snakes and ladders and he begins the game by rolling the dice.

"How can someone be snakes and ladders champion?" He asks, moving his counter four places.

"Pure skill!" I grin, "no one ever wanted to play me because I always won!"

"Today your run will end!"

"That's what they all said, Jonny, but they just couldn't do it. I fear you will suffer the same fate as them!" I roll my dice and move.

"Tell me about your work."

"Well, as I said earlier, I got made redundant from my job about eighteen months ago. I was a forensic accountant. It was a job I'd had since I graduated but the company was bought out and roles were merged. At first being redundant was the end of the world and I literally lay around eating chocolate and feeling sorry for myself. Paul got really ratty because I had no motivation to find a new job, but I didn't want to carry on with the same career. I didn't really enjoy it. I mean, it was easy, and I earned good money, well not like you, I earned enough, but the job just wasn't fulfilling. I knew there was more for me, but I had no idea what. Anyway, I eventually got out of bed and started redecorating the flat. I had redundancy money but without a job I had to be careful with it because I still had to pay my share of the bills. So I did everything as cheaply as I could. I made things, upcycled, scoured car boot sales and posted it all to my Instagram page, mainly for a record of what I was doing. Validation I suppose. Within a month my followers had hit twenty thousand, doubled the following month and now I am an interior influencer of sorts, I sell furniture that I've repainted, I travel all over the UK advising clients and I get sponsored by companies to market their products, although I'm really picky about who I work with. Ethics matter more than the sponsorship money. I love what I do. I am inspired every day. Redundancy was the best thing to happen to me."

"It sounds like you found your passion?"

"I really, really did. I couldn't go back to accounting now." I roll the dice and move up a ladder. "I am excited to get to work every day, before it was a chore."

"What does a forensic accountant do?"

"Find money, basically. Follow a trail to the missing pot at the end of the rainbow."

"Now, that is interesting." Jonny says.

"Not really. It wasn't a sad day to be made redundant."

"Well, I think it's interesting, because I have a missing pot at the end of the rainbow. I moved it somewhere when I was drunk, trying to hide it from my first ex-wife and I've no idea where it went. My accountant can't find it either and I wouldn't know where to start looking."

"I'll find it for you. Bam! That's one game to me!" I put my counter down on the WIN square with a flourish.

"Best of three?" Jonny asks, pulling a face.

"You're on!"

***

"I hate to say I told you so, but I told you so!" I laugh, putting two large potatoes in the oven.

"I don't want to talk about it," Jonny mutters in a faux grump, opening a tin of baked beans and emptying the contents into a pan. "What was left of my reputation has been damaged beyond repair."

"You lost five games of snakes and ladders, it's not the end of the world!" I turn the gas on and lean against the counter, picking up my red wine. I'm not entirely sure how many bottles of the expensive rioja we've had but my head is a little woozy and I've lost all track of time. I assume it's early evening, not that the scene outside would give any indication. The storm has raged all afternoon and we've been round the hotel twice taping up leaks. The two torches have dimmed, and we've still not found any more batteries, so we are now doing everything, bar checking the hotel, by candlelight. It would be romantic. After copious amounts of wine, it nearly is romantic.

Jonny is captivating. The melodic way he speaks is hypnotic and the stories he's told me are funny, heart-breaking and incredulous, in equal measure. He feels like a safe place, somewhere I can be myself which is making it harder to ignore the truth of my relationship with Paul. Part of me doesn't want the storm to end because it's easy to hide here but I feel drawn to Jonny and that is not a good thing. Not a good thing at all.

Jonny

Molly is lying on the sofa with her feet on the arm of the chair, gazing into the fire. I don't think I've been staring but we've got through so much red wine, I'm not sure of anything. Conversation has been easy, and we've laughed so much the cuts on my stomach hurt, but as the hours have passed silence has fallen. It's not awkward, just comfortable and calm. She makes me feel good, she's sweet and kind, non-judgemental and seems to like me for being me. It's unnerving. Once we got over the magazine article, it surprised me how easy it was to talk about my life, the things I've done wrong, the mistakes I've made. Molly just listens and then says something kind, and for the first time in years, I don't feel the weight of failure. I can learn a lot from her.

Her face is framed by candlelight, and it enhances the elfin features. She's so pretty, so natural and normal and the softness of her body draws my gaze. It wasn't that long ago that someone turning me down would have become a challenge that I would have eventually won, but already Molly is too special to be a challenge. I feel like I have finally met my best friend and with someone like her on my side I wonder if I could walk the long road back. I ignore the niggling voice that reminds me about Chelsea, my wife who is probably hanging off another celebrity and splashing the images all over social media. I feel sad that she does it for the attention that she should be getting from me, she deserves better, the mess of our marriage isn't her fault, but I've blamed her. She needs to be free. I owe her that much.

Molly yawns loudly and turns onto her side to look at me. "You know, Jonny. For a day that started in the worst way imaginable it has turned out to be a great day! You were right!"

94

"I am on occasions!"

She laughs. "I think I may go to bed. I suddenly feel completely knackered. Do you mind?"

"Not at all. Take the torch with you, do you want me to show you to your room?"

"No, it's fine, I remember the way." Molly pushes herself up. "Thanks Jonny, for more than I can possibly say. I'll see you in the morning?"

"You sure will, sleep well Molly."

"You too," she says and picks up the torch. "Night Jonny."

"Night."

Molly hesitates for a moment by the door and starts to say something before she seems to think better of it and walks into the darkness. I fight the urge to follow her. It would do no one any good if I did, just add more complication to an already complicated life. The torchlight glows as she walks slowly across reception singing a song that I recognise. I'm not expecting the flashback of images that bombard me with the soft melody of the song – I'm standing on a stage, huge crowds, bass speakers thumping, lights glaring, looking out at a sea of faces that are singing back to me. I can smell the sweat, the smoke, the hot bodies, and feel beads of perspiration running down my forehead onto my cheeks, stinging my eyes but when the image fades it's not sweat, it's tears, my tears and the heat is from the wood burner close to my face because somehow I've ended up on the floor rocking back and forth and feeling a pain so intense throughout my being that I can do nothing but sob. It was real for a moment but all that is left is a broken dream and a fractured memory from another time and the only person I want to talk to about it, is Molly.

Tuesday

Molly

I can't sleep. The wind is screaming through the gaps in the windows and despite being wrapped up in the biggest duvet I've ever seen, I just can't get warm. The terrifying roar of the waves, so close to the hotel, seem to be shouting my name, as though they hadn't succeeded in their task and are still intent on claiming me. There is no way I'll ever be able to go in the sea again. Ever.

I toss and turn for a while but between the screaming, the hammering of the rain on the windows and the deep booms of the sea, sleep just won't come. My eyes burn with tiredness, but I give up and light a candle. The draught blows it out, so I move the candle onto a table in the middle of the room and try again. It stays lit.

What a day.

It's the sort of day that sounds too far-fetched to be real, but then they say that truth is stranger than fiction, and this has been the strangest, most traumatic experience of my life. It's also opened up more questions than my tired brain has space for, but I can't avoid listening to the thoughts that tell me that Paul just doesn't care and I'm not sure that I mind.

He resents me. He resents my job, the success and the money that I'm happy to share. My salary overtook his, and he hates it. Hates that my social media followers have exceeded his, that my YouTube videos are sometimes more popular than what he produces – there shouldn't be competition in a relationship, there should be mutual support and mutual pride, but it has only ever been that way if it has been about Paul. My support for him. My pride in him. I didn't ever notice before but now I can't see anything other than that truth and being here has made it too difficult to pretend otherwise. There isn't a future for Paul and me, and when I get home, our relationship is over.

Well, shit.

Eleven years.

I burst into tears. Damn it, I've not cried this much since I was a teenager. I can't keep the tears in, and my arms instinctively wrap themselves around my middle, holding me together. The guttural cries come from somewhere dark, beyond me, a combination of sadness and fury. I am sad - sad for the loss of the couple that we used to be, a couple who were so amazing together that everyone was jealous. They wouldn't be jealous now, they'd pity us. How long have I been pretending? I close my eyes, trying to steady my breath and stem the flow of tears but all I can see is the mammoth wave coming for me, the flipping of the car and the paralysing fear that I was going to die, all because Paul forgot about me.

Everyone is expecting us to get married, have babies, move to a village outside of Bath and be Mr and Mrs two point four, with our people carrier and two dogs. I can't imagine that scenario anymore and I know that it's not the future I want. I don't think Paul wants it either, which is why there wasn't a ring. I still don't know what I would have done if there had been, but I wonder if I wouldn't have been as aware of the failings in our relationship if I hadn't nearly died?

I try to picture how things would have been if he had proposed but there is a darkness that surrounds me when I try to fit myself into the image. Where do I go next? If there isn't a 'Polly' what is next for me? I close my eyes, taking deep breaths to ground myself and I let my mind float into emptiness. For a moment, it's peaceful and quiet and I wait for the clarity to come until the white wolf sits next to me, its strange silver eyes boring into mine. I feel my body jolt sharply and I'm back in the room. Oh no.

It's just the trauma, that's all, nothing to worry about, my meditation didn't mean anything. *Are you sure?* I mean, obviously I've noticed that he's very handsome and that he has the most incredible wolf-like eyes I've ever seen, and he's really nice plus he didn't mind that I threw up in his bin… but that it's. *Really?* Yes!

I find the torch, pick up the blanket from the sofa and leave my suite. Rather than stay in my room with my thoughts and send myself crazy, I'll find Jonny's money for him. There is always a path to the pot at the end of the rainbow, it's just a question of finding the right starting point. I'm certain that the piles of files and boxes of paper in his office, near the kitchen, would be the right place to begin. I'm not sure how far I'll get without access to the internet and banking systems but doing something other than listening to my inner voice will save my sanity, for now.

I cautiously walk down the stairs, gingerly feeling each step, wrapping the blanket around my shoulders to keep out the cold. The hotel creaks and groans under the battering it's getting from the storm as though it's begging for the bombardment to stop. I know how it feels. Alone in the darkness is almost as isolating as being alone outside in the storm. I pause for a moment, wondering if I should give up the idea and go back to my room, but being alone with nothing to distract me isn't what I need right now.

I make my way along the pitch-black corridor to the kitchen, stubbing my toe on a doorstop that the torch's weak beam misses. I swallow down the nausea. "Ouch, ouch bloody ouch," I mutter as I hobble the remaining way while pain shoots through my foot. Limping across the kitchen to fill a saucepan, I put it onto the stove to make a coffee and light the candles that dot the worktops before sitting on the stainless-steel counter to wait for the water to boil. The drip that falls from the kitchen ceiling into the bucket has worsened and several ceiling tiles have begun to rattle. Whatever Jonny may think about the building surviving is looking more like wishful thinking than fact.

Still, I like being in this creaky old building, with a lost soul for company. There is breathing space to be found within the damp walls, and in some bizarre way, I feel grateful for the time. I feel free. I've not called Paul back, my phone is still on the bathroom floor where I chucked it, and it can stay there because I don't want to talk to anyone anyway. I pull the blanket tighter around me and watch the water drip into the bucket. It's hypnotic. Rhythmical. Drip, drip, drip, drip, and the pan joins in - bubble, pop, bubble, pop, bubble, pop. There is music in the hotel, and I think that Jonny brought it here.

Coffee made, I blow out the candles and leave the kitchen, taking the dark passage towards the Jonny's office, which is the smallest of the three and, to my dismay, in more disarray that I had first thought. It's unsurprising that he wouldn't be able to find his missing millions buried in all the mess. I clear a space on the desk, knocking a pile of papers onto the floor and search for a notepad. Finding nothing, I walk into the larger of the remaining offices and find one in a cupboard, along with a pot of pens, taking them back to Jonny's office with me.

I lose myself in the paperwork. Time flies as I sort and file document after document. There are decades worth scattered around the office, some illegible, others mapping a direction for me to go in. His accountant is sloppy and unprofessional but there is a pattern slowly emerging. "It would be so much easier with a computer,"

I grumble, adjusting the torch. My eyes are hurting from working in the dim light, but it stops me thinking about anything else and at the moment that is a good thing.

I don't know how long I work for. All of the clocks stopped and the only one that doesn't need electricity is in the bar. I'm gasping for a drink but the coffee I made has gone cold. I drink some of it anyway and stretch out and do some sort of yoga pose that straightens my back out. "Take a break, Moll," I tell myself as I stand up stiffly, joints creaking. I walk down the corridor towards the bar, the torch omitting such a small beam that I have to take each step carefully. I pour myself a large glass of water and drink it down in one go. God, that's better, my throat no longer feels like the Sahara, and I let out a satisfied burp.

"Charming," a light comes out of the dark reception and shines at me. I hold a hand up to my eyes.

I giggle, "sorry, I drank my water down too quickly!"

"It's better out than in! Are you ok? You're up early!"

"Am I? What time is it?" I squint at the clock.

"It's around five am."

"Really?" I yawn and rub my eyes. "No wonder I'm tired."

"I thought you went to bed?" Jonny says putting the torch down and coming behind the bar. He reaches behind me for a glass and fills it from the tap under the counter.

"I couldn't sleep." I reply, watching him. He moves with the gracefulness of a dancer. It's intoxicating and I realise that is his power. It's why he has been as successful as the article said, because he has something that is so much more than natural talent. I don't know if it's aura, or pheromones or something more supernatural, but whatever it he, Jonny has it in bucketloads.

101

Unconsciously I take a big breath in. He smells citrussy, and musky – it's masculine and raw, not something that can be faked. It makes me feel dizzy. I step away. "I think I must be in adrenal overload or something, each time I closed my eyes I saw the wave coming for me, so I gave up on sleep and started looking for your missing millions.!"

Jonny looks a little startled. "In my messy office? You're brave!"

I laugh, "I really am! I've never seen a mess like it! I have to say, though Jonny, your accountant is rubbish! You could have had this sorted years ago!"

"Have you found anything?" Jonny asks, clearing his throat.

"Not yet but the paperwork you have tells a story. I'll have another look tomorrow. Or today." I yawn, "how come you're up at this time?"

"I couldn't sleep either so I'm going for a swim. Wanna come?"

"Where do you plan on doing that? On the driveway?"

Jonny laughs, "we have a spa and pool here! Fancy joining me?"

"I don't have a costume."

"Wear your bra and pants, I won't look!" I hesitate. "Besides," he says cheekily, "I've seen it all before."

***

It takes me ages to come out of the changing room. It's one thing to have been stripped down to my worst bra and bad pants to save my life, but it's another to willing strip off and display myself in said bra and Jonny's boxer shorts, which I've made smaller with safety pins from the first aid box. It will be just my luck that the pins work themselves free and the shorts float off, leaving me with even less dignity than yesterday morning.

The pool is in a converted chapel that is attached to the main building by a wide corridor with big arched windows that are being pounded by the rain. I imagine in daylight the chapel looks spectacular with stained glass windows sitting in the local grey stone, but there is little to see now aside from what is touched by the light from the candles that Jonny has lit around the pool. The sun should be coming up, instead there is nothing but the charcoal darkness outside. I look down at the inky water and shudder. I can't do it, I can't get in.

"Molly?" I hadn't noticed Jonny floating in the pool.

"I can't." I whisper, "It's too soon."

He swims towards me and hauls himself out of the water, but I can't do anything other than stare fearfully at the ripples. Jonny takes my hand and says, "I'll jump with you. I've got you."

"Have you? You won't let go." Tremors knock my knees together and Jonny squeezes my hand tighter.

"I won't. On three, ready? One, two, three."

We splash down into the water. Jonny keeps my hand firmly encased in his as we disappear under the surface. I wasn't ready. I was never going to be ready to jump. All I can feel is the wave coming down over the bonnet and the pounding of the water as it turned my car over with such ease. *I'm going to drown, I'm going to drown.* My legs kick frantically against the bottom of the pool but I can't swim. The water is too heavy, it's keeping me down. I don't know how long I'm under for but it's too long. I've been under too long. Oh my God, I can't breathe. I can't get up. I'm going to die. Death has finally claimed me. Then Jonny tugs my hand, pulling me upwards and I feel the water fall away as I break the surface.

103

I burst into tears. Again. Noisy tears that echo around the chapel. Jonny wraps his arms around me and I cry against his wet, bare skin.

"You've done it," he says, smoothing the hair back from my face. "You did it, Molly. You jumped."

"You didn't let go."

"I said I wouldn't."

"How long was I under for?"

"A few seconds."

"Really?" I take a step backwards in the water and he drops his arms. "Is that all? A few seconds? It felt like hours."

"I expect it did. Trauma messes with your mind."

"Is that what happened to you?"

Jonny gives a big sigh. "Yes," he says finally. "Shit that I thought I buried came back and that was that." He lies on his back and floats. I try not to stare but my God, even in the dim light his body is stunning.

For a man in his mid-forties, with a drinking problem and a hedonistic past, he is one beautifully proportioned man. I knew he had broad shoulders with muscles in his arms but there is a firm, hard, defined chest that I had my face against, that leads to a slim waist that leads to... holy moly a flat stomach covered in what looks like a strangely designed tattoo, and under that is a smattering of hair like a secret trail leading to... *STOP LOOKING MOLLY*, I almost yell at myself. *Stop looking. He's married, you're in something that resembles a relationship, you can't look.* My internal voice is screeching at me, shrieking louder than a harpy. If it had arms it would be shaking me and probably slapping me around the face right now. I'm trying not to look but my goodness it takes willpower I didn't know I had. He's probably wondering why I haven't said a word in response to his statement, but the truth is, I can't! My mouth has dried, and my tongue is stuck to the roof of it. I'm scared if I open it, I will drool.

Oh my God, I'm in pants and my worst bra and he looks like that. OH MY GOD.

"Moll?"

"Hmmm?"

"You ok?" I think he's grinning. His voice sounds as though he is, and he must know that not only does he smell amazing, he looks amazing too. He must be so used to crazy women going mute when he takes his clothes off, but damn it, I didn't ever think I would be crazy mute woman. I thought I was a tiny bit cool but clearly, I'm as cool as an over-fried chip. Damn it!

"Yep. Tip top," I lie and turn over onto my front to swim up the pool. Now I'm in the water I may as well swim, and at least focusing on swimming stops me focusing on Jonny's hot body. When I get to the end, I check the safety pins in the boxer shorts. Can't have them coming loose, especially now.

"Feeling better?" Jonny asks.

"Yeah, thanks for jumping in with me."

"You jump, I jump… isn't that a film?"

"Titanic." I say. "The film I have cried at the most out of every single film ever made."

"Really? Why?"

"Well, for starters I'm a sucker for a doomed love affair, and secondly, there was room for two on that door. He didn't have to die. It broke the heart of every teenage girl, and some boys, for generations!"

Jonny laughs, "really Molly, I don't think I've ever known anyone like you!"

"Oh, in what way?"

"Just sweet."

"Sweet?" *Sweet?* I'm admiring his hot body and he's calling me sweet. Maybe it's the universe telling me to

105

use my gym membership. "I'm not sure any girl wants to be called sweet!"

"Maybe not, but it's safer for you."

"Are we back there?" I feign an eye roll, not that Jonny can see, I'm too far away and it's too dark.

"You know it!"

"Jonny, I hate to tell you, but I am not one of those girls who would fall at your feet. I'm cooler than that!" *Yeah right!*

"You can tell yourself that as much as you like!" He's teasing me and I'm falling for it.

"Whatever, Jonny, but you're sounding egotistical and that's not a good look on anyone!"

He laughs and the sound bounces off the walls. "Yeah, I know, but it's been a while since I last had fun or laughed. How sad is that. I've literally been drunk for the past five years, longer really, more like twenty-five, and laughter has been missing. You brought that back. I'm pretty grateful you nearly died! Being here alone would have really sucked. I think you saved me from tipping over the edge."

"Really?"

"Yeah, but I wonder if I just needed to fall. You know, a wake up call, or something. Maybe I just needed you here to catch me." His voice goes softer and I swim over to him, no longer caring what I look like in my mix-matched underwear.

"And did I?"

"Did you what?"

"Catch you?"

"If I'd been here alone, I would have smashed into pieces, Molly."

"Oh." I don't know what to say. No one has ever said anything like that before. I've always been 'silly Molly' or 'party Molly' or 'one half of *Polly* Molly' but no one

106

has ever credited me with catching them before. "I think you caught me too."

Jonny

Molly is asleep on the sofa. In the candlelight she looks peaceful, although the dark smudges under her eyes betray the exhaustion she must have felt before she finally gave in to sleep. We swam for an hour or so at the time when the sun should have come up, instead the outside world stayed charcoal grey and the rain continued to smash onto the building. There was a calmness inside the chapel with only candle light, even for Molly despite her fear about jumping in. She's so brave. Much braver than me. I can't imagine anything getting in her way.

I tuck the blanket tighter around her and top up the wood burner and leave the bar. Wandering around the hotel, checking the windows and doors, I feel lighter than I have in a long time. I've had fun. I've laughed and I have forgotten how it feels to be in the company of someone who doesn't have an ulterior motive.

She's easy to be with. It worries me. Soon she will leave, and the lightness will be replaced by the familiar darkness and I'm not sure how easy it will be to go back. She said the hotel gives her breathing space but for me, it's just a noose to slowly suffocate myself. Or maybe she's got post-traumatic syndrome, because as I told her while we were swimming, no one ever likes being here.

The hotel has sprung more leaks in the hours that I slept. Damn it, it's going to cost a fortune to repair. I pad leaking windows with towels from the housekeeping stores and walk through the lounge to the conservatory feeling dejected. The door rattles ferociously and the whistling wind screeches through the gaps. I'm hesitant to open it, and when I do the water floods in, soaking my feet in seconds. The antique glass in the roof has fallen in and the water has risen so much it's threatening the structure. I force the door closed but not before I'm drenched. For fucks sake. Goddamn this fucking place. Why did I fucking buy it?

"Jonny?"

"The fucking conservatory has caved in."

"Oh no," she says aghast. "What can we do? Can we repair it?"

"It's too dangerous. It's pretty much all glass and if that falls down and hits one of us…"

"Arse." She says yawning. "That isn't good news at all."

"I regret this hotel more and more each day." I mutter. "Such a mistake." I lock the door, using my body to push back against the wind.

"I think you need to change your mindset. I think this hotel could be fabulous." Molly stretches and I try not to notice that the tee-shirt rides up over her soft midriff.

"That's because you haven't seen it in the daylight!"

Stop it, Jonny.

"I'm serious, Jonny. This hotel could be awesome, you're just seeing it in the wrong way. It just needs some love…and a little drying out!" Molly grins flashing the torch over the carpet. "It looks shit now under all the gloom and the damp, but once the storm stops and the insurance sorts you out, it'll be awesome. Honestly, with a little care this hotel could be a sanctuary for anyone who needs an escape. I told you that I feel safe here, like I can breathe, there aren't many places that make me feel like that, and I'm sure others will feel the same way."

"You must feel safe at home?"

"Home?" She gives a humourless laugh, "home has been more claustrophobic that I'd realised. It took nearly dying to realise just how much. I think I was meant to come here, to be here in the silence, with you. I think fate decided that I need to wake up. I kept the picture, you know. From the magazine."

"Why?"

"I don't know." Molly whispers, hanging her head. "I saw something in your face that I recognised. There was a sadness in your eyes that didn't fit with the jovial pose and I realised that I saw that same look in the mirror."

"Oh Molly, lovely, sweet Molly, don't keep it, bin it. You don't need a picture of me to see yourself, you're awesome! I'm a fuck up. The best thing you can do when it's safe to leave, is get as far away as possible and never look back."

"Jonny!"

"I'm serious. You don't need someone like me in your life, a fuck up…"

"Haven't you noticed? We all are fuck ups."

"Not quite like me." I say, my voice cracking. I have an ache in my throat, and my chest constricts painfully.

Molly stares me right in the eye. "I don't think you're a fuck up." She says, smiling softly, "we all get lost sometimes, and there is no shame in it. I couldn't even jump in the pool without you holding my hand, what does that say about me?"

"You're not quite like me, though Molly."

"The difference between you and everyone else, is that people know who you are. Mistakes are public. Normal people can make their mistakes without the world seeing. It doesn't make you any more of a fuck up than the rest of us."

"I lost my livelihood and you have built a business." I say sharply. "In this insane competition we're having, I think you win!"

"But it came at a cost." She replies, not meeting my eye. "A huge cost, and now I have to make a decision that will change everything." A solitary tear rolls down her face. "And when I think about it, I feel sick and scared and so anxious that I want to bury my head in the sand. That's not brave, that's fucked up."

I don't know what to say to make her feel better. All that is going around my mind is that she kept a picture of me, and I don't know what that means, or why it means so much to me. "What can I do?" I ask.

"Nothing," she wipes the tear away. "I'm just knackered and being overdramatic. I'm not usually like this!"

"Well, you did nearly die!"

"Yeah, that's true. And I feel all discombobulated with outside being so dark that I have no idea of the time. The clock has stopped in the bar, so I guess that's it, all normal rules no longer apply!"

"Normally I'd get drunk…"

"That sounds good, but I think I'd become way to miserable to be around if I did that. Perhaps I'll go and have another rummage in your finances, unless I can help you clear up this mess?"

"I don't think there is much I can do in here, apart from light the fire and hope it dries out. Any more leaks and we may be done for!" I try and be light about it, but I feel the blackness coming. I flash a grin at Molly, but it feels fake. I wonder if it looks fake. She doesn't seem to notice if it does.

"Then I'd better find that money quickly. You may need it if we set sail across the ocean! But first, coffee! Strong coffee because your office is enough to bring me out in hives!" Molly laughs and it's a bright, tinkly sound. Her face lights up, despite the bruise-coloured shadows. "Do you want one?"

"I'd rather have whisky!"

"Later, coffee first! It's …oh, I don't know, some time, or other!" She pulls a face. "It is so strange not knowing. Freeing in some ways and strange in others."

111

"How so?"

"I'm worried that my parents are worried, but I wonder if Paul has even noticed that I've not called him back, although I expect my phone has gone flat. I didn't think to look when I went up to brush my teeth. Maybe I should, in case it's still on and I can ring my folks."

"Don't you want to ring Paul?"

She shrugs. "Not particularly but I suppose I should. Do you want to ring your wife? I'll put the saucepan onto boil then run up and get it."

She disappears out of the lounge, and I can hear her footsteps padding along the corridor. Does Chelsea want to hear from me? Unlikely, but I should call her. Maybe. *You are disgusting. Irrelevant. Drunk. Has-been.* I wonder where she is, what – or who – she's doing and whether she has even thought about me. Do I want her to think of me? It would be nice to think she does, it would also be nice to think she has a picture of me somewhere, but I don't imagine she does. A photo would be too much effort. I sigh. It's not just Molly who has to make difficult decisions, I do too. The decisions that I've been drinking to avoid for the past five years can't be ignored anymore. I feel sick. It wraps itself around my insides, twisting and choking. Damn it, how the fuck did I get here? The voices whisper their cruel words, tormenting me, sounding like my father, his words, his vitriol, his hatred, his utter revulsion. *Shut up, shut, shut up.* I slam my fist down on the grand piano and the force of it hits hammers onto the strings, sounds that clash with each other. I can't breathe. I pull at my neck but the memories tighten against my throat until I can't get any more air in. *What will Molly think? W*hat does it matter what Molly thinks, the voice whispers. You're no one to her. You are just a place to stay. She has a life, a boyfriend, a business – when the weather improves, she'll be out of your life and she'll cast no thought onto irrelevant you, the broken, broke drunk who once gave her shelter. The black fog swirls around me and I feel the waves of self-loathing start crashing over me again as I sink into the darkness.

"Jonny? Jonny? What's the matter? Jonny." It's Molly's voice but she's so far away. Perhaps this is what death feels like – that real life just floats away behind you as you go spinning into the afterlife. Perhaps I am finally dying. Losing my words was the first step, the drink the next, then my broken marriage and now it's safe to go because of a stranger who came in from the rain.

"Jonny, can you hear me?" The muffled question sounds panicked but it's somewhere ahead of me, just out of reach. My head hurts. There is too much pressure inside of my skull and it's going to explode. Help me, help get out of here. Take me wherever I need to go, but please don't let it hurt. Please let it be quiet. Will anyone be sad if I go? I don't think so, their lives will carry on and they won't notice. I'll just be gone, no longer be the disgusting broken drunk, or the useless dad, or the terrible husband or *that fucking kid*. It will be as though I've never been here. Take me, it's fine, but don't let it hurt. I don't want any more pain.

"Jonny, look at me." The voice is coming from an angel, standing before me, bright, bright light surrounding her. She is holding out her hand, gesturing for me to follow her. She is safe. She is a safe place. It won't hurt. *I'm sorry* I whisper, *I'm sorry for all of it.* I can hear music. The angel has brought music. Someone is playing the piano. I know the song. It's soft. Gentle. Melodic. It doesn't hurt anymore. The pressure around my throat eases. Colours are more vivid, the blur around the edges has sharpened. The music still plays and I feel it, vibrating in me and all around me. I feel it. It's been gone for five years but I can feel it. She brought it back.

113

"How did you know?" I whisper, feeling tears on my cheeks. "How did you know how to bring me back?"

"Back?" Molly asks, her hands held above the piano keys. "Back from where?"

"I thought I was dying…"

"I think you had a panic attack. I didn't know what to do, because for ages you didn't respond and your eyes rolled around that I wondered if you were having a stroke, or a heart attack, but I remembered seeing a programme once about music helping with anxiety, so I tried it. I only know two songs on the piano, this one and chopsticks." She bursts into tears and half falls, half collapses onto the floor and wraps her arms around me. "What happened, Jonny. Are you alright? Oh my God, you scared me." She holds me and buries her head into my neck. Her tears soak my tee-shirt, but I don't move, I just let her cry. I can feel her heart beating against my chest and her soft body warming me.

Molly washing up on my doorstep is a blessing and a curse. I feel good being around her. It's been the strangest twenty-four hours of my life which, given my track record, is saying something. So, what now? What the fuck do I do now? *I kept the picture you know.* Oh Molly, why did you have to say that? I don't mean to, but I pull her closer.

I don't know how long we sit wrapped in each other, but it feels safe, and warm and real because Molly is real. I've always known when someone showed me affection to gain something from me, but Molly is completely different. She's hurting too but there is an authenticity about her, and she wants nothing from me, but my company. I am feeling things that I'm not sure I have ever felt before. In fact, I know I haven't and it's terrifying in so many ways. Once upon a time I would have bedded her and walked away, but times have changed and I'm not the same person I was. I've paid the price for my blasé attitude to others' feelings but even so, as soon as she can leave, Molly needs to go. I don't want to break her too.

Her tears have stopped but we don't let go. I can't seem to make myself move and when she buries her head in my neck it's clear she can't either. It bothers me that Molly makes me feel alive. She's making me feel things. She will leave a huge, irreparable hole when she goes.

"I think we should move," I say, not really wanting to but we've begun to shiver from the chill of the wet carpet.

"Yeah," she replies with a sigh. Molly unwraps her arms from around me and awkwardly stands up. She doesn't look at me, confusion flooding her face. Fuck, she's not supposed to feel anything for me, she is supposed to remain unscathed.

"I'm so sorry." I tell her as I stand too. "I'm such a fucking mess, Molly, everything is bubbling under the surface, and it won't go away. It's never gone away. It's just now that everything is really shit, and I have no purpose anymore, it won't stay hidden. For fucks sake, I'm so sorry, I'm not the sort of person you want to get mixed up with! I'm sorry you had to see that."

"Mixed up? What do you mean mixed up?"

"In my shit. You don't need that, I'm so sorry." Thank fuck, I've misread her kindness, it's just my feelings I need to deal with.

"There is no need to be sorry, Jonny. I've had my fair share of meltdowns. You should have seen me after I got made redundant – I was a skanky mess. It happens. We all have shit that we try and hide from. I've been trying to hide from what has been staring me in the face for ages, and just because you were famous… are famous," she corrects herself, "means a larger amount of shit. Do you want to talk about it?"

115

"I don't know. I've never been able to talk about anything. Too many people would have sold me out if I did." I pause, "although, they sold me out anyway."

Molly lightly touches my arm. "Well, I won't sell you out and I would never judge you. No one is perfect, especially not me." She grins, "stylish may be," Molly twirls in my clothing and laughs, "but not perfect. Shall I help sort this room out before any more water comes in?"

"No, I've got this!"

"Ok, in that case I'm going to change out of these wet trousers and find your missing money." Her face falls when a loud beep omits from the sideboard. "That'll be Paul." She shakes her head, "I sent him a text to say I was alive, I bet that's his reply."

"You didn't ring him?"

"Nope, I don't want to speak to him at the moment, in fact, right now, I don't ever want to speak to him again. I've called my parents, I did that before I came back down, do you want to ring your wife?"

"Not particularly."

She chews on her lip and looks hesitant. "Maybe you should, just so that she knows that you're ok?"

"I doubt she'd care."

Molly reads the message and hands me the phone. "It's up to you. Feel free, or not, whatever." She leaves the room and I stand staring at the phone for longer than I should. Then I punch in Chelsea's number and wait for her to answer. She doesn't pick up before voicemail kicks in.

"Chelsea, it's Jonny." I sigh. "I guess you're out somewhere. Or not answering because you don't know the number. Anyway, it's just a quick call. The storm is a lot worse than they said it would be. It's so dark that I don't know if it's day or night and the sea is up to the front door...I don't know why I'm telling you all this

116

really. I only rang to say that my phone has gone flat, and I can't charge it because we've lost the electricity. I'm using a guest's phone, there is only one other person here, everyone else left when the weather warning went up to red. Anyway, I don't think there is a lot of battery left so there isn't much point in phoning me back." I pause and take resigned breath, "I know why you don't want to come here, Chels, and I understand, it's depressing, it's all been depressing but I think we need to talk. Properly talk. Soon. When the storm ends. You need to come here, and we can talk." I pause, "ok, I'll speak to you soon, when I can, uh, bye." I end the call and sit down heavily on the piano stool, causing the legs to squelch against the carpet. It's going to smell like wet dog in here. Fuck it. I slam my hands down on the keys, the sound erupting against the silence in the room.

"Temper temper!" Molly comes into the room, dressed in clean clothes and carrying a coffee. She grins at me. "I've made you a drink, if you're not too savage to drink it!" Her feet pad against the swollen carpet. "You can't get cross with the piano, it's too beautiful. Why don't you play something?"

"I can't." I mutter sharply. "If I could I probably wouldn't be stuck here…"

"Maybe you need to try. Maybe the reason that you had that moment earlier, was because you are denying the thing that makes you *you*. Maybe it's time to take a deep breath and do it. Just play. One note. Why don't you try? I'll sit with you for as long as it takes."

"Why are you so nice to me?"

She smiles, "because you are nice. Look, I've been in a shit, dark place too. It took months to come out of, but I did it because I went with my passion. The reason I couldn't motivate myself to get another finance job because I just didn't want to do it. No matter how shitty

117

Paul got about me lying around like a slob, I couldn't make myself apply for the jobs. In the end I just listened to what my inner voice was telling me, and I went for it."

"You don't want to know what my inner voice tells me."

"After what happened today, I can well imagine what it says. You're better than the voices, Jonny."

"How do you know?"

"I have a sixth sense about these things. I feel…" She stops and takes a breath. "Ignore the voices, Jonny, and everything that says you can't, or puts you down and makes you feel shit. Just go for it. It's there for the taking. You don't lose a talent like yours…"

"How do you know I have talent? Have you ever heard anything I've done?" I hold her gaze, her blue eyes sparkle at me. She makes me feel as though I can do anything. There is no side to her, she's just kind. She may be the first person to ever be genuinely kind to me.

"Actually, I have, as it happens. I used some of the remaining phone battery to find you on YouTube! Oh my God, your voice is incredible. It gave me goosebumps. You can't let go of that Jonny, I can't imagine what could have taken it all away from you."

"Then I shall tell you." I say, standing up and holding out my hand, "but not right now because I'm starving. Besides, it smells of wet carpet in here."

"Funny that," she replies with a smile.

Molly

Jonny makes scrambled eggs, and we sit in the bar with plates balanced on our laps. The wood burner is roaring but the room has more of a chill and the step between the bar and the lounge is showing signs of damp. The storm has to end soon, before the hotel is reduced to a single brick, yet I'm worried about life on the outside, about the decisions I've made and am yet to make. I'm comfortable here, with Jonny, a man who seems so broken and in despair, but I know I am safe with him. I don't feel as though I need to change who I am, which is good, I've done so much of that without even realising.

The resentment I feel towards Paul is sitting like a weight in my belly and I don't like it. I don't want it there. It aches. I don't know how to get rid of it, without compromising on my anger. I'm allowed to be angry. I am here because he didn't give me a second thought. I'm allowed to acknowledge that, but I don't want to hang onto the weight, it's black and tarry although if I'm honest, it's not just because of the situation I've found myself in, much of it is directed at me. I allowed this. I gave away my power. That's on me.

Jonny is staring into the flames, lost in thought. He is so handsome that I keep unconsciously gazing at him and I worry that he'll catch me. Which would be really embarrassing! Right now, he doesn't seem aware of anything other than whatever is going on inside his head.

I wonder how he ended up here. What pushed him from fame and fortune to almost nothing. He doesn't seem to have deserved it, although I don't know anything about him, beyond the magazine article and his kind hospitality. Maybe it was deserved. I will only ever know his version, but I don't get the vibes from him that he is a bad person, just lost and regretful, something I recognise in myself.

I didn't lie when I said his voice gave me goosebumps. I've not heard a voice like his – raw, smoky, gravelly. It was a voice I could just listen to on repeat and never tire of it. If it had a smell, it would be oak and whiskey. It's a voice to fall in love with. *Goddamn it, Molly, you can't think things like that.*

Except it's true.

It is *the* voice, and there is something about him that is going to make leaving that little bit harder.

It all feels very confusing - the absence of light, of time and of the world outside and my life. It's not the same as it was two days ago. Everything is different. Somewhere beyond the bar something slams, a door probably and I'm reminded of the apocalypse outside.

"I feel like I'm in a movie where I'm being chased by something dark and dangerous, except in this case it's the sea." I say, forking up the remaining morsels of egg. "I still think it's coming for me, and your hotel is suffering because I beat the sea yesterday." I grin, "although I sound like a freak saying it! I watched a film once where these kids' beat death, except death couldn't be beaten really and got them all in the end."

"You're cheery!" Jonny laughs, turning to look at me. In the firelight his wolf eyes glitter orange. "I think you watch films that perhaps you shouldn't!"

"Yeah, that's true! When I had my slobby months, I watched everything the streaming service had to offer - Christmas films, vampire series, horror films, kids' films, reality shows – I was pretty warped by the end of it!"

"I can't remember a single tv programme that I've watched in the last five years."

"Not one?" I ask incredulously.

"Nope! I was either drunk or thinking about getting drunk or just staring into space and losing hours being miserable. It's no wonder my wife spends her days hanging off footballers' arms and avoiding me."

"She sounds delightful."

"She's a victim really, taken out by my massive fall from grace. She isn't a bad person, she just can't help me because she doesn't know how. She married a superstar and ended up with a failure. I'd go out with footballers if it were the other way around."

"Would you?" I ask, "or are you just making excuses for her, because it's easier than admitting that she could be the wrong choice?"

"That's deep."

"I nearly died, I can be deep!"

Jonny laughs and puts his empty plate on the table, then leans back in the chair and rests his head on the back. "Is that what you've done? Made excuses?"

I want to say no. I want to tell him that for our whole relationship everything has been perfect, and it is only the past year where it's gone wrong. Only, that's not true. "Yes. I made excuses after excuses without even noticing I was doing it. Tiptoeing around Paul to keep his ego stoked, making sure he felt top dog and never talking about how well my business was doing in case it upset him. I can't believe I did it but perhaps it's down to my past and because of that I never noticed how little he prioritised me. It crept up and I just didn't see. It's probably more my fault, than his, I should have bigged myself up and made him listen."

"Hindsight is a wonderful thing," Jonny says gently. "If I could have seen how I ended up, perhaps I wouldn't have shit on everyone."

"Did you really shit on everyone?"

"Women, I definitely did. I used them and left them. I was a wanker."

I lean forward in my seat. "Were you though? There were a group of girls at uni who went out on Saturday nights just to bag themselves a rugby player, or football player and if they weren't successful then they hit the clubs and went for the rich men. They knew exactly what they were doing. Sometimes they had a short relationship, other times it was one night. If the men were famous, they went to the papers and pocketed the cash... they were just as much of a shit as the men who took advantage."

"You didn't want to bag yourself a celebrity then?"

"No, I was way too scruffy for anyone famous to notice me! I went out in whatever I had on, plus I've always been slightly too chubby for body-con dresses and hot pants. I'm not a clubber, I like the pub. Jeez, I'm boring, aren't I?"

"I don't think you're boring," Jonny says smiling gently, "I can't think of a better person to be stranded with! You're very different to women I've met over the years. Your outlook is a complete contrast."

"I've had therapy and I still do a lot of work on myself, particularly since I was made redundant. I've definitely grown as a person, well, not completely because I'm still messy and chaotic and a little slobby so there is still more to do, but, you know, I am different. I have more belief in myself, and I think that's why I can't go onwards in life with Paul. Although now I've got to process the feelings I have about it, and that seems pretty monumental, even in the safety of this hotel. So, you see, I may not be a famous-person-shagger but I'm far from perfect."

"You seem pretty perfect to me." Jonny says simply.

I feel my face burn and I can't look at him. "You could do with giving yourself a kinder time, you're very hard on yourself. I'm not sure you deserve that."

"You don't know me."

"That's true, but as I said, I have a sixth sense. I think it's from all the yoga and meditation I do, it helps me see people clearly."

"Is that right?"

"Maybe!" I laugh. "Maybe I'm just talking shit!"

"I'd better do another leak tour of the building then I think it's probably whisky o'clock!"

"In that case, I shall go and do battle with your office! Can I use that torch? The batteries have gone in mine, and I don't know where they're kept."

"Sure." Jonny hands me the torch and our hands briefly touch, sending a spark ricocheting around my body. I leap back like a scalded cat, holding my hand to my chest. Jonny's wolf-like eyes bore into mine. There is a fire in the silver that holds my gaze like a rabbit in headlights and a warmth spreads through the middle of my belly. A warmth that momentarily stops breath in my throat. It's a feeling I've never had before and suddenly I feel really vulnerable, as though everything single thought I have in my head is on full show. Oh hell.

"Uh, see you later." I mumble and stride across the room to the reception rubbing my hand as though burned, not daring to look back behind me. *Oh no, Molly, no, no, no.*

Jonny

"How are you getting on?" I ask Molly, walking into the office. She has lit a couple of candles and is sitting on the floor with a pad of paper and files piled up next to her. I don't dare hope that she will find something in the paperwork, but somewhere out there is ten million pounds and I'd very much like it. I must have jolted her from her thought process because she jumps when I speak and the file on her lap falls to the floor.

"You've been at this for hours," I say, crouching down beside her and taking the torch. "You must be knackered." She looks really cute, brown hair spiked in all directions and pencil marks on her face. The torch that she has clenched under her armpit is just about giving enough light to make out the scribbles in the files.

"It's a bit of a buzz actually," she says not meeting my eye. "Although my bum has gone to sleep." She yawns. "I know I said it before, but your accountant needs firing."

"Do you want the job?" I grin.

Molly rubs her eyes, "God no! My days of making sense of paperwork are gone."

"What's this?" I ask, pointing at the pad.

"It's a map, in a way. Each file leads to a new file, like a destination. It's just a question of piecing it all together to get to the pot of gold. I'm onto something though, my Spidey senses are tingling." She rolls her shoulders. "I feel really stiff, time to move. I'll have another look tomorrow…assuming it's still today?"

"I've no idea!"

"What's happening outside?"

"Well," I sigh, "it's still raining, the lounge carpet now has puddles, the leak in the kitchen is a downpour, the back corridor is flooded, and a window is broken in one of the bedrooms. Pretty shit, but it could be worse."

"Oh man," Molly says, putting the pad and file down and awkwardly standing up. "I'm beginning to think this storm will never end."

"It will, then you can escape."

"I didn't mean I wanted to leave, I just want a break from hearing the thrashing sea continuously, it freaks me out. God, I feel like an old lady." She says, as her knees creak, "and I'm starving, and strangely in need of a large drink."

"I've got a pie in the oven and a bottle of red wine open!"

"Music to my ears," Molly stretches out, the tee-shirt tightening over her breasts. *Stop staring Jonny.* She's not really looking at me and even in the soft candlelight, there is a flush spreading over her cheeks. I thought it was just me who felt the zing in the bar, but I'm pained to realise it was her too. Damn it, Molly, you need to get away from me. I've had so many women over the years but none that ever felt like a friend or made me want to protect them with every fibre of my being. As much as I want Molly to forget she ever knew me, the idea of her going back to Paul makes me feel sick. I don't want her to go back and stay with him. *You want her to stay here? With you?*

Fuck, fuck, fuck it's all so complicated.

Molly blows out the candles but stumbles over a pile of papers as she turns. Time stops as I catch her mid fall, wrapping my arms around her slender frame and pulling her closer to me. I don't think I breathe as she freezes, looking up at me. God, I want to kiss her. Neither of us move, but the flush on her cheeks darkens and my heart thumps against my chest. What if I do? What happens next? Molly bites down on her bottom lip and I realise that the same thought is going through her mind. Oh fuck, are we crossing the line? I've been over the line a thousand times, but never with someone who really mattered, like Molly matters. I don't know why I've not kissed her yet, it's not as though Chelsea and I have any future, but I can't. I can't move my head down. *You don't want her to cross that line, you feel too much for her.*

Slowly, I raise her body, until she's standing. She won't look at me. Fuck. My heart sinks faster than a defective elevator and the already cold room gets colder.

"Molly?"

"What?"

I don't really know what to say. The atmosphere is uncomfortable, and the heavy silence between us has quietened the sounds of the storm. "Are you ok?"

"I don't know."

"Will you at least look at me?"

"What for?" Her eyes are glistening and she's gnawing her lip. "You don't need me to look at you, Jonny, you don't need anything from me."

"You're wrong, Molly. I need you more than you realise."

She takes a shuddering breath in, "I can't imagine why."

"Because I think you may be my safe place."

"You don't even know me, Jonny. I could just be another woman to sell you out."

"But you're not." The pause is long, and I have the fear that somehow, I've blown the first genuine friendship I've ever had.

"No," she says eventually, "I'm not."

"Come and get some food," I say, moving towards the door.

She nods and follows me along the corridor to the bar. It's the only room that now has any heat. The lack of windows makes it a sanctuary from the hammering, banging and whistling as the storm looks for any way in it can find.

I pour Molly a glass of wine and she downs it in one, holding it out for a refill.

"Thirsty?" I ask wryly.

"Something like that," she replies.

Molly doesn't knock the fresh one back, instead she puts it on the table and sits on the sofa, curling her feet under her. "Do you have any idea what time it is?"

"No, but the radio is on in the kitchen, there'll be a news bulletin at some point."

"Do you not have a watch?"

"It needs charging."

"Oh."

"Molly, do you want to tell me what the matter is?"

"There isn't really anything to tell." She takes a long breath in and reaches for the wine glass on the small table. "I don't think it will serve any purpose to figure out what it is, besides it's probably just cabin fever, or something."

She's lying.

I leave her watching the flames and walk along the corridor to the kitchen. The torch is omitting only a weak beam making the blackness seem more hostile. I stop at the housekeeping room to find batteries, then continue towards the kitchen.

The pies smell great. The rest of the kitchen, however, smells of damp and the bucket that I have been using to prevent the ceiling leak from spreading, is full. It has a festering seaweed odour that seems to spread even when I tip it down the sink.

I turn up the radio and start chopping vegetables, for the first time in longer than I can remember, my head bobs in time. It's pop, some cheesy boy band, and not the sort of music I would ever like, but the rhythm is catchy, and I can almost feel it vibrating on my skin until the voice in my ear says *you're a fucking piece of shit, boy.* I knock the chopping board onto the floor and pieces of carrot skid over the tiles.

"Jonny?" I hadn't heard Molly come into the room but her face fills with concern. "Are you ok? What happened?"

"Nothing, it was nothing, I just knocked the board."

"It doesn't look like nothing, you're really pale, even in this light."

"It's fine, Molly." I snap.

She looks taken aback by my tone but rather than say anything further she picks up the board and the knife and sweeps the carrots into the dustpan. I watch her cross to the fridge and take out the veg tray. "This is all looking a little limp now. Maybe we should cook it all."

"Maybe."

"Or not." She shrugs and puts the tray down on the counter. "If I was a good cook then I could make suggestions, but beyond roasting some and making soup with the rest, I'm all out of ideas. Something in that fridge smells a little off."

"Two days of no power will do that."

"You know what, Jonny? I think I'll just go to bed."

She slams the knife down on the counter top and strides out of the kitchen. *For fucks sake, Jonny what are you doing? You're being a total tool. Go after her, explain. Tell her everything. Just don't make things harder by being a dick.* I check the pies and turn off the oven, wrenching open the door and putting the oven tray onto the top. Then I run from the kitchen and catch up with Molly as she is crossing reception.

"Molly? Wait, I'm being a dick. Sorry. I'm really sorry. I have ghosts in my head and every time I let the music in the ghosts slap me down. I'm sorry. Don't go to bed, have some food, you must be starving. I'm starving. Come and eat with me, please don't go."

"Things feel weird, Jonny. I feel weird, and you're being weird. I don't even know you, so I don't know how I know you're being weird, it's just... you are."

"I don't mean to be." I say softly, "I don't want to seem like that to you. I just have spent so long burying my shit and for some reason this storm has flung it all back up. I'm sorry you're the one having to see it, it should be Chelsea..."

"I thought you said she was more interested in footballers."

"She is."

Molly chews her lip, "probably just as well I'm here then."

"You have no idea."

Molly

Something has happened between us, and I don't like how it feels. There is the overwhelming sense that everything has gotten weird since he came into the office. I honestly thought he was going to kiss me and when he didn't, part of me felt painfully and embarrassingly rejected. Which is dumb because, of course he wouldn't kiss me. For one thing, he's married, for another he's famous, and talented and really, really handsome, but fuuuuuuck, I wanted him to kiss me and then…gah, it's not even worth thinking about it. I'm not a cheater. I'm still with Paul, even though in my heart it's all over, but I'm not going to do anything that makes me feel that I've cheated. That's not who I am.

But I wanted it to be.

Damn it. Now everything is strange, and I'm confused. I need to get out of here. The storm, the isolation, the man – it's a combination of those things that are making me feel out of sorts and nothing to do with the strange silver eyes and the rugged, handsome face that I can't help but stare at.

I don't like it. I shouldn't feel this way about a man I've just met, a man who has complex demons and a drinking problem. I shouldn't want to know more about him, to know what makes him tick. What I should do is put some distance between him and the unnerving thoughts I'm having. He is married and, until I get home, I have Paul. I need to stop thinking about Jonny in this way. To him I'll just be another fawning fan-girl - a name to forget like all the others.

Shit.

"I need tequila." I say leaping off the sofa and scanning the bar for a tequila bottle with the torch as I walk over to the drinks. "And, before you ask, it's medicinal."

"Medicinal?" He raises an eyebrow.

"Yep. I plan to drink and drink until I can't drink anymore."

"I didn't have you down as a tequila girl, more prosecco or something." Jonny says lightly, although the candlelight picks up the confusion on his face.

"I'm not. I hate tequila."

"So why have it?"

"Because it feels like the right drink."

"The right drink for what?"

"To get absolutely hammered on." I brandish the bottle. "Come on Jonny, you can be on lime and salt duty, this tequila won't slam itself!"

✳✳✳

"My insides are burning."

"Tequila will do that to you!" Jonny says, filling up my glass. "It's not a drink for everyone."

"I bet you've had tons of it in your time."

"Not really, whiskey has always been my poison."

"How did you get here, Jonny. To this place? This moment? How did you stop singing?" I'm drunk and my subtly went with my sobriety.

Jonny looks down at the hand gripping his glass. Maybe he shouldn't drink if it sets of a spiral of angst, but he seems completely in control as he raises the glass to his mouth. I stare at his lips. Perfect, full lips, surrounded by days' old stubble. They curve up at the corners as though once he used to smile all the time but has since forgotten how to. He is so handsome. Probably, *the* most handsome man I've ever seen. It's like someone designed

131

a man based on every woman's dream and Jonny was the result.

Or maybe I'm just drunk, and he doesn't have silver eyes dotted with topaz flecks. Strangely hypnotic eyes that I'm staring into. The tequila has slowed my movements and I can't take my eyes away from his, but I think he's staring at me too.

Someone coughs and it breaks the spell. Jonny shifts and run his hand along his jaw before he pours more tequila. The moment could have been in my head. It could have been a second, not a long, lingering look, I'm not sure I can tell the difference now. I try to focus my brain into sensible conversation.

"The article called you part of the lost generation of rock. How lost is lost?" The brain focus didn't work.

Jonny looks startled and the hand round his glass turns white. *Shit,* I think, *I shouldn't have asked that.*

He looks beyond me and into the darkness. "I've been famous for over twenty years. Properly famous but I guess you can say that I had infamy beforehand. I was always going to be *someone,* not a fucking despot failure like my dad. He was a drunk who used to beat me and my Mum regularly. He beat her so badly that she nearly died. That's when the police moved us, and we didn't see him again. I was seven or eight. We were lucky. There wasn't the same sort of help then as there is now, but we got away from him. I had my leg in plaster and my Mum had a broken nose, ribs and a fractured jaw, but the Police and the Doctors worked their magic, and we left town in the middle of the night. The nurses gave us a few items of clothing from the lost property bin. One of the kids on the ward gave me his action man, and we went. Mum was treated at a hospital in Manchester, and I stayed with a foster family until she was well. Then we were moved into a flat. It wasn't a great flat and the area was rough,

132

but we were finally safe, and that's where we lived until I was sixteen."

Jonny closes his eyes so tightly they scrunch up into slits. I quietly pour more tequila, but he doesn't touch it. I don't think he even sees it. Jonny is trapped in the past and I can see the anguish on his face. I want to reach out for his hands, but they are so tightly clenched that tremors travel up his arms. I couldn't imagine a life like that for a child, to be so terrified of the person who is supposed to protect you and when I picture it, I want to be sick.

Jonny opens his eyes and looks at me, giving me a tight smile. "My Dad found us eventually. I had just been signed to my record label and was being touted as the next greatest talent. He sniffed us out from the hole he was buried in, told me he was sorry, that I had brothers and sisters from some other poor woman, and he was proud of me. Then he went crawling on hands and knees to my mum. Of course, he just wanted money, not her but she fell for it and went back to him. After ten years of being safe, she went back. He probably broke her again. I don't know." Two big fat tears roll down his face and get caught in his bristles. "I made her choose and she chose him. I changed my name and made up a whole new history." Jonny wipes his face and looks at me, the rawness of what he has just said flashes in his silver eyes. "She went back to him, Molly. After he nearly killed her. I can't explain the pain of that, it was worse than the broken leg and the beltings I got. I've never told anyone that. No one knows my story. I stopped existing and became someone new."

I reach for his hand. It's warm and soft and holding it gives me a fizz in my belly. "I won't tell anyone."

"I know." He says simply. "In forty-five years, you are the first person I've ever trusted. It doesn't make any sense, I don't even know you, but I feel as though I've

133

known you forever." Jonny sighs, "and I'll confess something to you," he says squeezing my hand, "this is the happiest I've been in years, but it bothers me so much."

"That doesn't make sense, or perhaps I'm more drunk than I thought! How can you be happy but bothered?"

Jonny sighs, "because this friendship is on borrowed time."

"It doesn't have to be."

"I think, sadly, it does."

"Why?" My voice catches in my throat when I consider what it means. I feel as though the safety of this isolated hotel is going to be ripped away from me, and I'll have no choice other than to go home. I didn't think I'd stay here forever, my life is in Bath, but I didn't think I'd be a friend for a storm, and not beyond that. If I'm honest, the idea of never seeing Jonny again is like a brick sitting in my lungs, preventing me from catching my breath.

"I'm not someone you need to be friends with, Molly. I bring sadness and heartache wherever I go. You know how I ended up here, with nothing. That doesn't happen to decent people."

"Of course, it does, you're talking shit. Things happen to decent people all the time. I'm a decent person and shit has happened to me. It doesn't mean it makes it ok to break up with a friend, you're just feeling sorry for yourself. It's self-pity."

"Self pity?"

"Yes."

"That's harsh."

"Probably, but it's also true. You have an amazing talent, Jonny. You're a superstar, I mean, how many people get to where you've been? Selling out stadiums and breaking records. Not many. I could probably count them on one hand but most importantly, you got there in spite of your parents, in spite of them letting you down so despicably they should be rotting in jail. Even though they were the worst of the worst, you still made it. It makes me really sad that you lost it all, because you are a superstar, and the world needs you."

"The world needs me, does it?" Jonny asks bitterly. The coldness in his voice shocks me. "It needs me so much that it left me here to rot."

"You brought yourself here to rot."

"You know nothing." He snarls and knocks back the tequila, pouring another as soon as the glass is empty. He doesn't pour me one.

Jonny

Her words have cut deeply, so deeply that I can almost feel them bleed. Maybe she's drunk, maybe she's right. Maybe it hurts because she's just told me the truth that I've been hiding from. Have I just blamed my father for all this because it was easy? Did it give me a reason to succumb to the Imposter Syndrome I've had since I was eighteen, giving it a voice and letting it in?

I wish it was as easy as that. I wish I could believe that the world did want me, that my talent was enough but all I can see is skinny, broken, unloved little me, and I am lost in a past that I have tried so hard to forget. A past that has never, ever gone away. No matter how many hit records, how many sold-out stadiums, how many women, how much whiskey – it never went away. I have always been the scared little boy watching as his mum got beaten by his dad, unable to do anything to save her. I never, ever wanted to be like him, but DNA is a strong link even if the emotions aren't there. *Irrelevant. Broke. Broken. Drunk. Disgusting. Failure. Has-been* and the voice that rings so loudly it may have been uttered in the space next to me, *don't forget whose son you are, boy.* I've never been able to forgive my Mum for going back to him. I begged her not to, but she went anyway. She didn't even give me a backwards glance as she walked out the door. I don't know where she is now, or even if she is alive. And the last time I saw my dad, I wasn't in the room long enough to find out, just there long enough for him to irreparably damage what was left of me...

"Jonny?" I've forgotten Molly is here. I move slowly to look at her and her face is filled with worry. She's worrying that she said too much, but she said the truth. She is a good person. Better than me. So much better than me. I was right to say that she didn't need a friend like me, I break everything I touch.

She gives me a soft smile and I feel the corners of my mouth curve up a fraction. She is so pretty that I could look at her all day. Molly has a light that surrounds her and when she reaches for me, she passes the light to me, and I feel warm. She's been in my life for mere moments, but she feels like a safe place. For the first time ever, I feel safe. It's been thirty-eight years since my dad nearly killed my mum. I should be over it now, and I hate that I'm not. I hate that I am still so terrified of my father and because of that he was able to take my words, my music...He took it all.

"He broke me." I say to her, looking down at her hand over mine, "my father. It was the biggest night of my life, a concert on my fortieth birthday, the biggest crowd ever by a solo rock singer and I was on a high. Such a high. I didn't think I would ever come down. He got let in somehow and before I went out to do an encore, he told me not to forget whose son I was. I changed my name so he'd never find me, but he did. And he broke it all. One minute in his company and BAM," I slam my fist onto the table, making Molly jump, "the music just left me. I hadn't long been married to Chelsea. She was living her dream life being Mrs Rock Star, somebody that people took notice of. Our marriage began to crumple when there were no more songs. She kept spending, my accountant couldn't find the money I'd hidden, so everything had to be sold to pay the bills..." I shake my head at the ridiculousness of it. "Chelsea keeps spending because it makes her feel good, but eventually there will be nothing left."

"I'm sorry I accused you of being self-pitying." She mumbles, "on reflection that was the wrong word!"

"Perhaps, but you just may have been right."

***

Molly makes us huge bowls of pasta for dinner. We both sway a little as we carry it back to the bar. The screaming wind still hasn't let up and the kitchen ceiling is now bowed under the weight of the water. Something else to put right, but tonight I don't feel the same hatred towards the building as I have. There is a tiny shift in my thoughts, tiny but it's there.

The bar has become a sanctuary. For one thing, it's quieter in here than any other room and the soft glow of candlelight, and the warmth of the wood burner, makes it seem a million miles from the storm. I know what Molly means when she says she can breathe. I can too, and I owe it to her. Despite her telling me truths I don't want to hear, she has been good for me. The little waif that washed up. I'm not sure I'll be the same person I was when she goes. I meant it when I said the friendship was on borrowed time. I think I could go beyond friendship if she stays too much longer. There is a thin line and I am balancing on it, and if I fell over, I would take her with me, and she's much to good for someone like me.

I stab at the pasta. It tastes good and the coffee that we wash it down with takes the edge off the tequila. It's been a strange day, long and difficult at times, but in so many ways it's been a great day. I look over at Molly, but she looks lost in thought as she eats, her mind somewhere far from the hotel. I wonder what she's thinking about, but I choose not to ask. I'm not sure I want to know.

The silence is good. It's calm. My thoughts are quiet. Something has shifted and it feels good. For the first time in years, I have hope.

✳✳✳

I do my third walk of the day around the building, checking that the windows and doors are still holding against the storm. It's not looking great for some of the floors, the windows have sprung more leaks than the Titanic and the meagre items I have to block them aren't going to hold. Still, it will buy us some time, I suppose, but the squishing of the carpet under my feet makes me fear for the floorboards. It will just be my fucking luck that the ceilings cave in. Molly thinks this place could be sanctuary and I'm trying to see it, but it's late, it's dark and it's bleak. I need to check the insurance policy, which I feel certain is in the General Manager's office. It's unlikely anyone would have trusted it to me. If the insurance is poor, the hotel may be just left to ruin. If I'd not gotten smashed that night, I wouldn't be in this mess, *but you wouldn't have met Molly either.*

I feel knackered. I caught some sleep this morning, but it wasn't enough. We are living strange hours, and now the clock in the bar has stopped, the time means nothing. Outside is still the dark grey ominous colour that gives no indication of whether its night or day, and the deafening sound of the sea throwing itself down onto the slope outside chills my heart. We'd have to move to the top floor if anything happens further down here, but the ceilings… fuck, fuck, fuck, this storm has to end soon, it's not as though there's any fucking rescue boat sailing past.

I finish my checks and head down to the lounge to check the conservatory door. Molly is in there playing the piano. It's the same song she played earlier but there is no panic behind the chords. She is just playing. She plays well. It's a song I know, a song from happier times and a warmth spreads through my belly and flows into my veins. The feeling of music, sounds and vibrations that

139

have guided me my whole life, the feelings I lost, are coming back. Molly is bringing them back.

"Do you know this song?" She asks, "it's the only one I know. I had a friend at school who was amazing on the piano, and she taught me this. Somehow, I've remembered it." Molly grins, "I know the words too, but I shan't terrify you with my singing voice, it's enough to shatter glass, and we don't need any more of that!"

"Yes, I know this song," I say. "I did a cover of it in…actually, I can't remember when, two thousand and five perhaps, I know it was in America, on some tv show I recorded in LA. There was a campaign for me to release it, my record company wanted me to, but it never felt quite right. I love the song though, I just don't think it suited my voice. Maybe I should have, who knows!"

"Do you miss singing?"

"Every single fucking day."

"So why don't you sing? It has to still be inside you, somewhere. Why not try and get a hum out?" She continues to play, moving back and forth in time.

"I can't Molly."

"Can't, or won't?"

"What difference does it make? Singing isn't an option for me anymore." I snap at her, "you know that. I told you what happened."

"You're giving your dad all the power. Take it back, it's yours. It's your talent. Why don't you try? There's no one here but me. Try and see, you may surprise yourself."

"I can't, Molly. There isn't any going back, it's gone. Over. It's not who I am anymore."

"Of course it is," she says loudly, pushing the keys more firmly. "You don't just stop being that person because your parents are evil arseholes, Jonny. Take it back, it wasn't theirs to take away. It's yours, it's always been yours."

"I don't think you listened to anything I said. Fuck it, I'm going to bed," I say sharply, my tone so cutting that it abruptly ends her playing. "Good night."

Molly

He just leaves and I'm left all alone in the darkness. Damn it Molly, you total cretin. Why say those things? Why go on at him, he said he was broken so why did I ignore that? I slump my head onto my arms, resting them on the top of the grand piano. *Talk*, I said, *it's good to talk*. Perhaps he wasn't ready. He certainly wasn't ready for my psychobabble.

Fuck.

I close the lid of the piano and stand up. I don't particularly want to go up to my room if he's gone that way, he needs space from me and my *therapy is good for you* shit. I clear the plates and mugs from the bar table, and, carrying a candle balanced on the top of the plates, I follow the numerous corridors to the kitchen. Putting everything in the sink, and lighting the candles on the counters, I run the water to wash them up. While the sink fills, I empty the buckets under the drips and look warily at the bowed ceiling tiles. This is going to be an almighty mess to clear up, nearly as almighty as the mess I'm going to face when I get home.

Home.

It seems a million miles away. Part of me doesn't want to go home, the other part of me really needs to be as far away from here as possible. I need to be away from Jonny. That's the truth. Fuck, what am I doing? Why am I thinking these things?

I leave the washing up soaking and take a fork from the cutlery tray crossing the kitchen to the dessert fridge. I sit down on the floor, propping the door open with my foot and pick up the gateaux. The icing has gone soft with the lack of refrigeration, but it still tastes pretty amazing. Comfort eating has become an all-too regular occurrence since I realised that Paul and I were not the happy couple I thought we were. I was spot on when I told Jonny we all had our thing. I liberally coat the fork in gateaux and shove it into my mouth. *I am disgusting.*

"Is there room for one more?" Jonny comes quietly into the kitchen.

"Sure." I gesture. I don't look at him. Jonny takes a fork and comes to sit on the floor opposite me.

"Sorry for the dramatics," he says. "I'm not sure what happened."

"I do." I say, spooning more cake into my mouth. "I'm a dick and I said dickish things. I should have just kept my mouth shut."

He shakes his head, "it was more than that, Molly. You playing the piano made me feel something I wasn't prepared to feel. It had very little to do with what you said."

"Sorry."

"Don't be."

I chuck my fork down onto the plate. "I can't eat anymore. I shouldn't have had it in the first place, it was a knee jerk reaction to feeling like a dick. I told you everyone has a *thing*!"

He grins, "your *thing* is definitely more appropriate right now than my thing, especially after all that tequila!"

"Tell that to my waistline," I tell him. "It's just as well there is growing room in these joggers."

"I don't think there is anything wrong with your waistline," Jonny says simply.

I blush in the darkness.

***

Jonny

I'm woken from a very disturbing dream about Molly, by an ear-splitting crash and the sounds of flowing water coming from beneath me. I fumble for the torch and leap out of bed, pulling on a pair of shorts and trainers as quickly as I can. Fuck, please don't let that be anything major. Rubbing sleep from my eyes, I leave the suite and bump into a terrified looking Molly. Her elfin hair is stuck up in all directions and she's chewing on her lower lip. She's wearing my boxers and tee-shirt and she's looks so breathtakingly sexy that it takes everything I have to not ignore the threat of disaster and pull her into my arms to kiss her as though my life depended on it. I've known many, many women. I've fucked many, many women but none that have ever brought out such conflicting emotions as Molly.

"What was that?" She asks, her voice trembling.

I can't meet her eyes because I don't trust myself.

"I don't know." I hurry to the top of the stairs and take them down two at a time. Molly is behind me holding her torch high.

"Oh fuck! No, no, fucking no."

Armageddon has finally struck. The sea has beaten down the front door and in the battle of the hotel versus the storm, the storm is winning. The water is flowing into the reception and slopping against the steps that lead up to the main corridor and the bar.

"Shit. Oh my god, Jonny. Shit." Molly grabs my hand, hers feeling small against mine. "We need to fix that door now." She says urgently, her voice trembling. "With whatever we can find to barricade it."

"I'm not sure we can," I reply looking down at the swirling water. "I think we are totally fucked."

"We have to try. If we're quick we may save the rooms we use. Otherwise we are completely screwed."

She's right. "I'll go," I tell her, "I don't want you to get into any harm…"

"It's fine, I can hold my own against the sea. It's ok. I'm ok." She speaks really firmly and lets go of my hand to start walking down the remaining stairs. I can feel how much she is trying to be brave. The only giveaway is the hard pull on her lower lip by her teeth. I'm pretty sure the idea of walking into sea water is a nightmare for her and I feel a heaviness in my stomach. Fuck. *No, Jonny, no.*

I run down in front of her and stand at the lowest possible step looking at the flooding. We have to wedge the door fast, otherwise we'll lose the lower levels to the sea and then we'll have nothing.

"Jonny, let's prop the door up and use the book case from the bar to keep it in place." Molly says her voice wobbling. "Or do you have another idea that would work better?"

"That would work fine, if we can get the bookshelf off the wall." I look around the reception. All the rooms and corridors lead from it, but they are all raised up by three steps. The reception is a strange shape, more like a circle with arms, which may just be the hotel's saving grace tonight. "Ok, I'm going to lift the door, can you move the desk?"

Molly holds her candle up, protecting it from the wind with her hand, and looks over at the desk. Her face fills with worry. It's a big, wooden desk, carved from an oak tree that was felled in the grounds. It's solid and heavy. Not as heavy as holding back sea water determined to get inside.

"Dump all the contents." I tell her. "That'll take some of the weight out. The safe is in it, once that's moved, it should be easier."

Molly descends into the cold water and shudders. "It's freezing. Now I know how Kate Winslet felt." She wades across the room, and I wade towards the door. It's been ripped clean from its hinges and the rain has taken advantage and followed the sea inside. The screaming wind blows all the candles out and I can hear Molly quietly start to cry. She's scared and I want to comfort her. My heart is pounding. I'm fearful of being swept away and leaving Molly here alone, but the sea isn't lying in wait for me. There are no freakish waves outside the door, just a mass of water flowing in.

There are splashes after splashes and sobs after sobs as Molly blindly empties the desk into the flood and I fumble in the dark, hands under the water, searching for the door. It's like the desk, carved from the same tree, and the weight of the water makes it nearly impossible to lift up.

"The desk is empty." She says.

"Can you help me lift this?" I ask, "I can't manage it alone, the water is making it too heavy."

She wades across. I can hear her breathing, jagged and shuddery, but she keeps her face turned away from me. It's too dark to see her expression but I can guess. She is terrified.

"Molly?" I ask, "are you ok?"

"Fine." She sounds anything but fine. "What do you need me to do."

"Stand here and hold this corner, I'll pick up the other side."

"Ok," she says in a small voice, "but be careful."

The water splashes me as I kick my way past her. I crouch down again and feel for the other corner. "Got it," I tell her. "Can you get a grip of it, and we'll lift it on three?"

"Ready."

"One. Two. Three." Somehow, with a kind of superhuman strength we wrestle the door up through the water. I can feel sweat on my forehead, from the exertion and Molly is groaning, but we get it clear, and I walk it back towards the frame. It takes an age, and the rain fights me with drops that feel like shards of glass. The cuts on my torso burn and pull, making me gasp with the pain. *Shit.* I ignore it and push the door up to the frame. With every ounce of strength I have left, I hold it in place.

Molly heaves and strains the desk over, gasping and groaning with the exertion but eventually she reaches me, and we barricade the door. It holds. Water seeps in around the edges but the worst has been kept out. There is nothing we can do about the flood in the room but for now, the rest of the ground floor is protected. Unless another door goes.

Molly pants. "We need to move the bookshelf before my body breaks," she says. "Maybe I will go back to the gym, there is something to be said for weight training!"

I laugh even though it makes the skin on my stomach hurt. "I weight train and it definitely doesn't prepare you for fighting with a biblical storm."

"Well, on a plus, I'm burning off that chocolate gateaux," she comments as we walk up the steps and through the lounge to the bar, "every cloud, and all that!"

We pull the books from the shelves and manoeuvre the bookshelf across the flagstones and into the reception. It takes both of us to get it through the water to the door and when we get there, Molly moves the desk. I push the bookshelf against the door and then we move the desk behind it.

"We just have to hope that holds," I say resignedly.

"It will, have faith." Molly says, "man, I could murder a drink. My heart is absolutely pounding."

"If it makes you feel better, I could murder one too."

Molly rubs her hands over her face. "I swear the sea is coming for me. How did it get up the hill? Perhaps it hasn't finished what it tried to start." She bursts into tears. "I feel like the building is losing its fight...I'm so cold but I can't face walking through all that water to go and get changed."

"Go into the bar and put the log burner on, I'll get some blankets from the housekeeping room." I put my hand on my stomach and wince. The pain in the cuts is excruciating.

"Why are you holding your stomach like that?" She asks sharply, "have you injured yourself?"

"A drink injury, nothing serious!" I move my arm to gesture that all is ok, but she catches it and flashes her torch at my stomach.

"You're bleeding!"

"It's fine!"

"I did a first aid course the month before I got made redundant, come into the bar and let me see." Molly doesn't wait for me to say anything, instead she walks up the steps to the bar and I follow her. She kneels on the floor and lifts up my tee-shirt, flashing the torch at my stomach. "Bloody hell, Jonny, I thought this was some weird tattoo design! What did you do?"

"I fell onto a bottle a few days ago."

"Did you get the cuts checked out?"

"No."

"Oh my God, you are so dumb."

She runs her hands over my stomach, "I'm just checking for any glass." Her fingers pad across my skin slowly, deliberately, and I feel a heat rise up my spine.

"Don't do that." I say, harsher than I should have. She ignores me and continues her check.

"It's ok, I can't feel any glass. Don't move, I'm going to fix you up."

148

Molly stands up and crosses the room to the first aid box at the back of the bar. She pours a glass of vodka and comes back to her seat on the floor. Opening the first aid box, she takes out some cotton wool, plasters and a lotion, putting them on the table.

"What's the vodka for?"

"To clean these before I put antiseptic on."

"It happened ages ago."

"It may have done," Molly says, "but we've been in sea water so I'm going to clean them before I plaster you up. How the hell did you fall onto a bottle?"

"It was a bad night."

"Hmmm," she frowns at the cuts. "They look really sore."

"They are."

Molly mutters, "probably shouldn't have been moving furniture."

I nod slowly, "probably shouldn't have been drunk in the first place."

Molly seems to subconsciously trace her fingers over my stomach, avoiding the cuts. She doesn't appear to notice that she's doing it, but the burning trail of that she leaves ripples my skin. I can't remember the last time someone touched me with such care, without wanting something in return. In all the years, and all the women, no one has touched me like Molly is now. No one has made my skin explode like the gentle stroke of her hands. Fuck, I've never wanted anyone as much as I want Molly.

She looks so lovely in the candlelight, the soft glow lighting her face. I sigh.

"Sorry, am I hurting you?" Molly asks, my sigh jolting her from her trance. She takes her hand from my skin, and I'm left feeling cold.

"No, not at all."

Molly dips the cotton wool into the vodka and daps it onto the cuts. It stings and I wince loudly. She ignores me and continues to clean the skin and the cuts. Once she's satisfied that she's cleaned them all, Molly smears antiseptic cream over my stomach and lays pads over the top, sealing them with medical tape.

"There you go, all done."

"Thank you."

"You're welcome," she replies wiping her hands on a napkin and wrinkling her nose. "That stuff stinks, perhaps avoid empty bottles from now on."

"Perhaps just avoid drinking."

"Maybe," she takes a big breath in, "and maybe I should avoid chocolate cake. It would make most of my clothes fit if I did!"

"You put yourself down too much," I tell her, standing up. "You shouldn't. You're hotter than you think you are!"

"Did you bang your head too?"

"Paul is a dick for not treating you right," I say, "I'll be back in a minute, I'll get some blankets."

✳✳✳

"They wanted me to do a reality show!" I say, resting my head on the back of the bar sofa and pulling the blanket tighter around me. My stomach is painful, with the cuts pulling on my torso.

"A what?" Molly wriggled up to sitting from her slump on the opposite sofa. We changed into dry clothes and the wood burner is throwing out a much-needed warmth. The two brandy glasses are far fuller than they should be. "Like the X-Factor? Or Love Island?"

"Some bullshit celebrity thing for has-beens to kick start their careers."

150

"Sounds hideous." She says tiredly. "I mean, I love watching them but going on one would be hell. Besides, you're hardly a has-been."

"I am these days." I reach for the brandy glass and hold it between two hands. I don't want to drink it. For the first time in months – years probably – I don't want a drink. I look over at Molly and catch her eye. She looks exhausted. Big shadows sit under her eyes and her skin is a sickly grey. "My manager dumped me, my wife is spending what's left of my cash and wearing tit tassels to flirt with footballers, I've got no words left and my hotel is flooded."

"It doesn't mean you're a has-been..."

"You read about me as a lost rock star..."

"Your words will come back, I'll find your money, can't do anything to help with the manager or the slutty wife though." She yawns loudly. "You cannot do a reality show, that's just desperate. No one respects anyone who goes on them, stay well away. Fuck them!"

I laugh and then groan.

"Is your stomach still hurting?"

"Like a bitch."

"Who'd have thought my trip to Cornwall would turn out like this. I was expecting to learn how to create culinary masterpieces and instead I'm drinking brandy in borrowed pants!

"If you had known, would you have still come?"

Molly takes a sharp inhale of breath and the wait for her to speak seems to take forever. When her reply comes it's simple and quiet. "Yes."

Wednesday

Jonny

The coldness of the bar wakes me up from a dream about my father. I have no idea how long I've slept, but I don't feel rested. I feel raw. My teeth hurt where I was grinding them, and my jaw clicks when I yawn. I've managed to squash my past down so why is it back to taunt me now? I don't have the strength for it. I shift on the sofa, but the wood burner has gone out and the blanket doesn't keep the chill away so wearily, I stand up, throwing it down onto the sofa. I stumble on the blanket that Molly was wrapped in. She must have put it over me after I fell asleep. That thought feels good.

I stand at the top of the bar steps, looking at reception. The water covering the floor smells of rotten seaweed and it makes my stomach curdle but with the rain still pounding the windows, there isn't much hope of getting rid of the smell. I do a few stretches to try and shake myself awake, but my body just groans and cracks and the cuts on my belly pull so I stop stretching and wearily trudge to the housekeeping store for buckets.

I think about this strange reality as I grab buckets, mops and cloths from the store room, which is stranger than any other time of my life and I've been to some very strange places. It isn't a reality that could have been written - a storm, a waif, a faded rock star, an empty hotel - but then the truth is always stranger than fiction. The idea of two people who would have never ordinarily met being thrown together by a bizarre twist of fate is ridiculous but is more real than anything I've ever experienced. The alternate universe that we have found ourselves in is oddly comforting but it's a place where real life doesn't fit. The trouble is, I can't go back. I can't live the life I was living, because it was a cold, empty existence shrouded in darkness. I can't go back because if I did, there would be no Molly. Fuck. As soon as the storm ends there will be no Molly. A life without her. How do I live in that world?

It takes effort and considerable deep breaths to walk into the freezing water which is slimy against my legs. I wade carefully through it to the window and push it open. The rain doesn't seem as heavy this morning and there is a lightness to the grey. Perhaps the storm is blowing itself out finally. *Then what?*

I try to focus on the task in front of me, scooping up water into buckets and throwing it out at the rain, but my thoughts continually drift back to Molly. She is the sweetest person I've ever met, and life will be so empty without her cheery demeanour. I've never known anyone like her, someone brave enough to turn a difficult situation into something to be so proud of and achieve it without any support. It's a shame that her boyfriend can't see what he has in Molly. What a dick. She deserves someone so much better than him. *Like you.* No, I'm not good for her, I'd just bring her back down. She needs someone to support her, be proud of her, share her successes. *Like you?* I wish it was me, but I'm too messed up to be the person she needs.

In my determination to never again be the terrified little boy I've become a terrified man and now it's too late. I am my father's son. There is no redemption for me.

"Hey!" Molly says coming up behind me. "Are you ok? You look like you've seen a ghost."

"Only the ghosts of my thoughts!" I smile, shaking off the mood I'm sinking into. "Is that fresh coffee I can smell over this stench?"

"Yes! Pan boiled, coffee brewed, it's in the bar! I'm strangely liking these olden times way of living. Although, a little concerned that I've got a laptop floating

154

in the sea with an inbox full of emails that I need to look at." She yawns widely and waggles her hand at the flood water. "I woke up trying to work out how we can get the water out but went to your office instead and now you've beaten me to it with the buckets. You're doing good! I'm loathed to ask if I can help!" She grins and wrinkles her nose. "It smells like festering fish. Maybe we should put masks on and go at superspeed, you know, before we get sick."

"Sick?"

"I watch the movies! People always get sick in dramatic situations." Molly wraps her hands around her throat and pulls a strangled face before laughing. Her prettiness takes my breath away, and with her elfin hair sticking up in all directions and a faint flush on her cheeks she looks so natural that I just want to stare at her forever.

"Oh, so what would Arnie or Bruce do then?" I ask giving myself a mental shake.

"They would drink their coffee while it's hot!"

"Coffee?"

"Hmmm," she muses, "well they'd probably have whiskey in all honesty, but it's too early for that!"

She turns on the step and I follow her into the bar. She's laid out cereal and what remains of the fresh milk.

"Most of the milk was off, and I'm a little concerned that the profiteroles I found in the dessert fridge may be about to go off too!"

"We'll eat those for lunch!"

Molly laughs, "that's what I thought." She pours two coffees from the cafetiere, tops them up with milk and hands me one. Then she fills a bowl with cereal and milk and sits down on the chair. Her creamy thighs cross, one over the other, and I try not to notice that my boxer shorts have pulled tight over the soft mound between her legs.

Molly has no idea how desirable she is, and I suspect she would laugh if I told her. Vanity is not something she seems to be afflicted with and her boyfriend doesn't sound like the sort of man who tells her. I feel conflicted – on the one hand she is the only person I've ever wanted to talk to about the things that I carry with me. That's a hell of a responsibility for someone I've only just met – and on the other hand, I want her as far away from me as possible. I have a need for Molly that terrifies me. It seems to be a need that is not just physical, it's mind and soul too. She is way too good for someone like me and I would break her like I've done all the others. *How do you know? Because I break them all.*

"I think we may be on the last candles." She tells me, crunching her cereal. "Although, I don't know where to find any more."

"There should be some in the restaurant, I'll have a look." I sit down on the floor and lean against the sofa.

"We probably need more batteries for the torches too because it will be pretty eerie when we have no light at all," Molly says gloomily. "Unless this bloody storm ends soon."

"It's definitely lessened overnight. It's lighter outside and the rain isn't quite as bad as it was. You may be free soon! What will you do as soon as you can get out?" I ask her. The coffee she has made is strong, but it's needed. I feel exhausted, mentally and physically, and the cuts still sting. I could sleep for a week, and it wouldn't be enough.

"I'm pretty scared of the lights going on and seeing my reflection in real life! Candlelight makes everything look so much rosier!" She laughs, "in real life? I don't know really. Looking forward to seeing the sky, and the sea where it should be and your eyes! You have the most amazing eyes and I'd like to see them in real life…"

156

Molly falls silence and looks down at her cereal bowl. My heart skips a little at the honesty. Damn it, Jonny, stop.

There is an embarrassed silence. Molly chews on her lips and plays with the spoon in her bowl. I want to say something complimentary back because there is a lot I could say, but it would just complicate everything so instead I say, "my mother has the same eyes as me. She used to tell me that we were descendants from the wolf priestess! She was an amazing storyteller and words came so easily to her but looking back I think she made up stories to take us out of the violent life we had."

I start talking about the night my father came home enraged that he had lost at the bookies that he threw me across the room so hard and I saw stars for days afterwards. I must have been six years old. I can remember the desperate look on my mother's face as he went for her, his belt pulled from his trousers, and folded over to cause maximum pain. She was begging him, pleading with him to not hurt her so that she could look after me, but rather than relent, my father stuck his boot into my belly with such force that I passed out.

"It's what I've done over the years," I tell a visibly shocked Molly. "Stuck my boot in emotionally. I was never going to be him, Molly, and that's exactly who I've become." I rake my hands through my hair and cup them over my face. "I am just like him. Knowing that and admitting it is worse than losing everything, worse than being rejected by my wife and my manager, worse than letting my daughter down and worse than being forgotten. The hate I feel when I look in the mirror because of what I've done and who I've been...Fuck, Molly, I never wanted to make anyone feel as shit as I did, and I have. I made them feel shit."

157

"You are not him, Jonny. You are you. Why would you assume that taking advantage of the opportunities that came your way makes you like him? The boys at university screwed anyone they could, do you think that they are beating themselves up about it now? No, they won't be, and neither will the girls who went out looking for a rich man. You are blaming yourself for what happened to you – for the way your parents treated you and for the way some of those women used you because of who you are. I can't imagine that you had to talk any of them into it."

"No, not usually." He says quietly. "I never really came on to anyone, they mostly came on to me."

"And the ones who didn't?"

"I could be very charming when I wanted to be!"

"I can imagine!" I giggle.

"Yeah, I always dumped them afterwards, so not that charming. God, Molly," I grip my head between my hands, "I don't want to be like him."

"You are not him."

"Why does it feel like I am? He never goes away. His voice is in my head all the time. All the fucking time. There has never been an escape, even when I made it, even when I had sold out tours, number ones and more awards than I knew what to do with – he was always fucking there. I changed my name, but he still found me and broke me all over again."

He was never going to make me cry again but I can't help it. My body shakes with a violence that I remember only too well as great wracking sobs that explode from me. He's in the room with me. I can smell his rancid breath as he leans over me, telling me I am a worthless piece of shit, that I am nothing, that I am an unwanted little fucker who ruined his life by being born. I try to keep the feelings in, so Molly doesn't see just how much

158

of a loser I am, but they explode from me in a cacophony of painful sounds that echo around the bar. I can't hold them back. It's a roar and a wail and a shriek and a cry - a barrage of painful, shattering sounds that rip through me, tearing at the cuts, at my muscles, at my bones and my insides, hammering against my brain that unleashes a tidal of memories that I don't want to remember. Me, crumpled in a heap beside the sofa, trying not to cry for fear of angering him more and my mum, my beautiful mum beaten and battered on the floor, in so much pain that all she could do was whimper while he pissed on her.

"She went back." I croak, my throat so tightly constricted I can barely breathe. I become conscious of Molly sitting over my lap, arms tightly around me, her head on my shoulder and a hand stroking the back of my hair. "He beat us over and over, but she went back."

"It's not your fault," she whispers, moving her head so her cheek rests on mine. Her breath is cool against my ear. "You were a child, nothing that happened was your fault. You mum made a choice, and you couldn't have done anything to stop her. We all have ties that bind us, and her ties were linked with your dad, whether they should have been or not. It was her choice to go back and nothing to with anything you did. You are not your father, Jonny, you are you. Amazing, talented you. You have a gift, and you have to choose to use it again because it's in you. The music is still there, the words are still there, you just have to want them enough."

"I'm so scared." What sort of man is scared? What sort of man am I that I could cry like a baby in front of a woman I don't know? I'm everything they said and more. Every harsh word that Chelsea, Susie and the endless other women have flung at me over the years, I'm everything they said. "What if I am all those bad things?"

Molly puts her hands on my cheeks and holds my face gently. "What if you're all the good things?"

"No one has seen the good things. It's hard to believe I have any."

She pulls me closer. "You are all the good things, Jonny." My head falls onto her shoulder, then Molly begins to sing a lullaby. She is safe, my angel. Until the storm ends, she is my safe place.

Molly

I don't know how long we sit for. Jonny is trembling and I have the strangest need to protect him with my whole being. His arms are tight around me, and mine equally tight around him, daring the world to try and break in to reach him. He mutters something about not being a man, being weak and pathetic, but I just hold him tighter as though to show him he is anything but those things.

Jonny shifts and I move, letting go of him and moving backwards to lean against the table, my coffee and cereal are forgotten.

The only sounds in the bar are our breathing, mine slow and steady, Jonny's more ragged and tired. We may be safe in this quiet room in the centre of the old building, but the storm has ripped the emotional bandages away and the wounds that kept our truths in, are gaping open. Jonny's are bleeding with a tidal flow of memories that he has kept locked away. My truth is nothing more than acceptance – I don't love Paul, but that's fine. Paul will be ok, he's handsome, he's been a pretty good boyfriend until recently. Someone else will make him happy and he'll be great for them.

I'm not sure how fine I'll be when I leave here though. Jonny has said over and over that I need to be away from him, but when I think about it, I get a pain like a punch in the gut. How is it possible to fall for someone in such a short space of time, in the most absurd of circumstances and for it to be completely wrong but feel so right? How has this happened? Is it fate winding me up because I survived the storm? I wish I had someone who could tell me what I need to know.

"Jonny?"

"Yeah?"

"Are you alright? Do you need anything? Whiskey? More coffee? Some food?"

"I don't know. I'm sorry Molly, I'm sorry that you keep seeing this shit. I don't know why it's coming out now." He rakes his hands through his hair. "I thought it was all just something I had to live with, but it's not as buried as I thought."

"It's good to get stuff out, Jonny. You can't hold onto all that, eventually it will just eat you up. Trauma stops being trauma when you take its power away. Well, that's what my therapist said, although she was referencing my stuff and its different to what you've been through."

"You're so wise!"

"I'm not really, I just learned through practice. It took a lot of therapy to sort things out."

"Things?" He asks.

I sigh and wrap my arms around my middle. "My boyfriend died when we were sixteen. One minute we were talking on the phone and arranging to meet at a friend's party that evening, the next I was getting a phone call from his dad to say he'd died. It was like I was sucked into some sort of phantom zone, I just stopped functioning. I sat in one place, without moving a muscle, for days because my whole body completely shut down. My parents were going nuts, they didn't know what to do, the doctor was talking about putting me into a teenage psychiatric ward and I couldn't say a word. I just sat there. It was horrific. It took me years to get to a place that I could move on." I shake my head.

"I'm sorry your boyfriend died, that's really sad. What was his name?"

"His name was Corey." I smile sadly as an image of him floats into my head. "He was my first love. I thought I was the luckiest girl in the world to be going out with him. He was the life and soul of school. Everyone liked

162

him and when he died there was an overwhelming sense of loss, not just our year group, but most of the school and it took a long time to ease. His funeral was packed, people had to stand outside the church because there wasn't enough room. Corey was so clever, he wanted to be a doctor. He would have been too. I missed him every single day. I still miss him. I miss who he was. I miss his smile and his 'you can do it Molly' comments whenever I had a wobble about a test or a hockey match – whatever it was he was always cheering me on. I am still so sad that he never had the chance to do all the things we talked about. He would have a been an amazing doctor…" I fall silent.

"What happened?" Jonny asks reaching for my hand.

"He went mountain biking with friends in the woods and fell off his bike. He smashed his head onto a rock and that was it. One minute he was there and the next, he wasn't." Jonny's hand tightens around mine and I watch as my tears plop down onto his skin. He doesn't wipe them away. "It took me a really long time to get over him then I met Paul, and he hated bike riding, so it felt safe to try a relationship again. Except I even compromised on talking about Corey, so maybe it was wrong all along."

"How so?"

"Paul didn't ever like me talking about him, he couldn't find the empathy to listen and over time I just stopped trying. I even stopped ringing Corey's mum on the anniversary of his death which now I can't believe I did. Corey was my first everything and he deserved to be remembered. I've never thought Paul would be jealous of him, I mean, he was dead, and I'd moved on but perhaps he was."

"Or he was being controlling?"

"Or that. I can't change the fact that I have been shit but I will ring Corey's mum when I get home, apologise for being so rubbish and maybe take her out for lunch, or something."

"That sounds like a really positive thing to do." Jonny says, lifting my hand up to his mouth and kissing it. We both freeze and he drops my hand as though it was a burning coal in his palm and a flash of worry crosses his face. I chomp down hard on my lip. *Don't say anything, not a word.* "Maybe I should get therapy," he says eventually. I'm glad for the change of subject although my hand is still on fire from where he kissed it.

"You should, you have to trust someone to help you."

"I trust you."

"That's nice to know."

"It's something to think about." He yawns and lies back on the sofa. "I'm so fucking tired. I think I've been tired for five years."

"Have a sleep."

"What are you going to do?"

"I don't know, I'll think of something."

I cover him with a blanket and watch his wolf eyes close. I pause for a moment looking down at his handsome face and I wonder how life will be when he's not around. Fuckity fuck fuck, this was not meant to happen. I make myself move away and walk to the top of the steps that lead down to reception and look at the flood. Jonny has done a good job of clearing some of it, but the water still sits too high. I head down the staff corridor and set a pan on to boil. Once it starts bubbling, I make a fresh cafetiere of coffee and put it onto a tray with milk, sugar and biscuits that I find in the larder, and the chef's little radio, before carrying it all back. I turn the radio on and pour the coffee, looking unhappily at the miserable task facing me. *Well, come on Molly, in you go.*

I wade across the floor to prop the reception window open as wide as I dare, although the rain isn't anywhere near as bad as it has been. Jonny was right, the sky has definitely lightened to a paler murky lilac and the sea sounds much further away. I guess it means that I'll be leaving soon.

"Stop thinking." I say crossly to myself and scoop the water up in buckets. It stinks. There is film of slime on the top of the water that wraps itself around my hands when I lower the pail into the flood. "Urgh, gross, gross, gross." The music helps distract me, and I sing along to the songs as I scoop and throw, scoop and throw although every so often the rotten-seaweed smell makes me gag. It's tiring work, but not tiring enough to stop me thinking about Jonny. Everything feels confusing and my hand still burns from where he kissed it. I don't think it was his intention to confuse me, but even so, I'm trying not to think about him, or his face, or his lips, or the hard body under the soft skin. I don't want to think about him in any way other than a friend, or as the man who saved me from drowning. It's too complicated and life is complicated enough.

"How are you getting on?" Jonny asks, splashing across the room to me. "Sorry you've been doing it all, I bet you're knackered now." He yawns widely and looks around the room. "If I had a year of sleep, I don't think it would be enough. Do you want to stop and have a rest, you've done loads."

"No, I'm good, other than gaining a stoop from all this bending!"

"It looks even lighter outside than it did earlier," he says scooping up a bucket full of water, "that's good."

"Yeah," I throw water out of the window, "It's so much quieter that it feels unnerving."

Jonny leans out of the window. "The sea has gone right back, although the lawn is in really bad shape. I wonder if the insurance will cover the garden too." He brings his head back in, "thank you, Molly."

"What for?" I ask, flinging my bucket down and stretching out my back.

"For just being there, for not judging, and for knowing what to do." Jonny says, looking down at the remaining water. "I don't know why all this shit is coming out now."

"You don't have to thank me," I say quietly.

"I do." Jonny says, taking my hand. "Because you are the first person I've ever trusted."

I smile, looking into the soft silver of his eyes, "that makes me feel so good. Normally anything I say gets disregarded so it's nice to feel like I've done something that made a difference."

"Your boyfriend is a fucking idiot."

"I think the fucking idiot is me." I pull a face.

"How so?"

"Talking to you about Corey has made me realise that I let Paul get away with so much because it took a lot of work to get to a place where I could have another relationship after Corey died. Like you and Chelsea, I think Paul and I were both victims of my past. It doesn't excuse things, but it suddenly explains a lot. Paul was everything Corey wasn't, and that's why our relationship started. He was supposed to be a one-night stand, but there was a safety in him being so different." I sigh, "I didn't have to supress the loud, messy, cheesy-music loving version of myself, I guess I chose to. I could have argued back but I didn't."

"It doesn't explain why he doesn't support you now though."

"No, you're right, it doesn't."

We fall silent. I bend down and start scooping again. Jonny joins me and eventually we clear the water from reception. The floor is littered with sand and strands of seaweed, but we use the mops to soak up the remaining water then sweep the tiles clear.

"That was more exercise than I've had in years," I laugh stretching my back out. "At least the mouldy fish smell has gone."

"Or you've just got used to it." Jonny says, throwing the mop down. "I think we're done here Molly. Let's get a drink, or five!"

"How about a Snakes and ladders rematch?"

"Not a chance!"

***

I have a quick shower to rid my skin of slimy sea water and sweat. It feels good to have the hot water rain down on me, and to use all the expensive body scrubs that fill the bathroom. When I'm finished and my body smells of lavender not manky fish, I wrap the huge towel around me and cross the suite to get the clothes Jonny has left for me outside the door. Under the clean scent of fabric conditioner, they smell of him and I hold the clothing to me, breathing in deeply. *Molly, have you lost it?*

Definitely.

There has to be a reason for all of this - trauma, isolation, two people thrown together – those sorts of things can seriously mess with a girl's mind. *Yeah, yeah whatever, Molly!*

When I get back downstairs, Jonny is lying on the sofa reading the magazine that he features in, by torchlight. His hair is wet from the shower, and he is wearing a tour tee-shirt of a band I've not heard of.

"Hey." He says, smiling and putting the magazine in his lap. "Feel better?"

"Loads! I can't tell you what a gross colour the shower water turned when I stood under it! Yuck, can you imagine what we were standing in?"

"I would prefer not to!"

I laugh. "Are you learning about yourself?" I gesture to the magazine.

"It was so much easier to read this shit drunk, but actually the guy is a total cock." Jonny throws the magazine on the floor. "For a start, he wouldn't know rock music if it slapped in his face, and secondly, he doesn't have a fucking clue."

"What about?"

"What happened. He just makes assumptions."

"Let him, Jonny. Perhaps one day you'll tell your story, but for now, fuck them!" I say savagely.

He eyes me, "you're ferocious!"

"You'd better believe it!" My stomach makes an almighty grumble.

"Are you hungry?" Jonny asks with a grin.

"Starving. Shovelling water will do that! I'm going to create something, prepare to be surprised."

"Can it be edible?"

"No guarantees," I say, taking one of the torches and flouncing off to the kitchen. Jonny's laughter follows me.

I like his laugh. It's deep, musical and warm and it makes me feel sad that he hasn't had any reason to laugh for years. *When was the last time you laughed?* It was a few months ago when I went out for cocktails with Ella. We hadn't planned on a messy night but that's how it turned out and the next morning I thought I was going to die from my hangover. I am messy, it's part of who I am, and it's been really hard to try and mould myself into being a different version of me. I wonder if Jonny is messy like me or tidy like Paul, who has everything in its place, neatly labelled and categorised. I shake my head,

Jonny is nothing like Paul but in some ways he reminds me of Corey. Jonny would be ok with me missing Corey, I sigh, and soon I'll have to miss him too.

I open the fridges and take out boxes of vegetables. Some of them have gone limp with the lack of refrigeration so I sort them out the best that I can in the minimal light and start chopping. I put them into the oven to roast and turn on the little portable radio. There isn't a lot of signal but I eventually find a pop music station. The music is delightfully cheesy, and I sway along to the songs as I rummage around for produce to make a meal.

I've forgotten how freeing it is to sing and dance with wild abandon. I've not sung since I started working from home, especially to cheesy tunes like the ones that are coming from the tinny radio. *For fucks sake, Molly, turn that shit down* was what I faced on a daily basis. *Jesus, Molly, your voice could shatter glass, can you shut up, I'm trying to work* every time a song I loved came on the smart speaker. And I did, I shut up, I turned it down, and then I stopped listening to music altogether. Goddamn it, Molly, what the fuck happened to you? So, I turn the radio up as loud as it will go, put a pan on to boil for pasta and I sing at the top of my voice. I'm so engrossed in singing, I don't notice Jonny come into the kitchen, until he stands in front of me.

"Oh my God, you scared me!" I hold my hand to my chest. "Jeez man!"

Jonny laughs, "you looked like you were having the time of your life!"

"I love a good sing song, but oh fuck, were you standing there for long? Did you hear me?"

"Loud and clear!" His silver eyes sparkle as he looks at me, and his smile reaches from ear to ear.

"Crap!" I slap my hands over my face. "No one ever needs to hear me sing, especially you!"

"I won't tell!"

"Good!" I take my hands down from my face and move behind Jonny to shake the oven tray. He turns the radio down a little and checks the bucket.

"It's nowhere near as full as yesterday, that's good." Jonny empties the bucket down the sink. "I am going on a leak check, unless I can help in here?"

"Nope, I've got this." I pause and listen to the radio. "Oh, I love this song. Can you turn it up?"

Jonny pulls a face. "Really? This song?" He turns the dial, and the tinny radio gets louder.

"Yeah, this song. It reminds me of nights out with Ella, such good times…" I start swaying. "Come on Jonny, dance!"

"I'm not dancing to this shit!" He laughs, "this isn't music."

"Of course it is, it's the best band ever!"

"Band? You need a lesson in music, woman! This isn't a band, it's manufactured shite."

"You have no idea what you're talking about! This is a great song, a great band…just great! Let go of your heathen thoughts and put on your dancing shoes!"

"No idea about music? Wash out your mouth!" Jonny feigns offence. "Do you know who I am?"

"Weren't you in a boyband in the early nineties?"

"A…a….a…what?" Jonny fans his face dramatically with a tea towel. "I cannot stay here for a moment longer and listen to this profanity!"

I laugh, "you know you want to! You want to dance and shake it out, let go of your *proper music* self and find your inner dancing queen!" I start swaying to the music, "there is no one to see you, and I won't tell that you danced to a boy band! Come on Jonny, live on the edge!"

"If I dance to this, I'll be falling over the edge!"

I find my groove and swing my body around the kitchen, singing along to the cheesy music as loud as I can. Jonny watches me with amusement on his face and leans against the worktop, arms crossed. I grin as his head starts to move in time with the music. "I bet you wished you could sing like me!"

"If I sang like you, women would throw rocks at me, not their lacy pants!"

"Now, now, Mr Raven, jealousy is a terrible thing."

He laughs and I grin. I love that I have no self-consciousness around him. I suppose it's not hard given the state I turned up in and the worst bra-and-pants combo that he was subjected to, but also, that I feel so free here. No phone, no internet, no sense of time, this battered old building and its battered owner have, in many ways, given me back to myself. I am changed. I won't be going home the same as I came down. There is a strength in me, a flame that has begun flickering in my soul that I know will turn into a raging fire over time. I think Jonny has saved me in more ways than one.

I hold out my hand, "Come on Jonny, dance with me!"

Jonny lets out a dramatic sigh. "Ok, if I must!"

He takes my hand and swings me around. We dance the most ludicrous of dances and the laughter fills the room. I double over when Jonny does an exaggerated boy band dance. "Stop! Stop, I can't breathe!"

"How can you listen to this shit?" He asks, sashaying up to me.

"Because it's fun." I grin, "and now I've seen you dance to it, you can never again market yourself on a moody rock star persona!"

Jonny laughs, "if I ever get the chance to be a moody rock star again, I'll be sure to add this song into my playlist."

"Oh my god, I'd love that! I'd buy tickets just to see you go all boyband on stage! Oooh, could I duet with you?"

"In my fantasy show where I sing manufactured pap, yes!"

"Good evening, Wembley!" I say dramatically, down the nearest wooden spoon, "let me hear you roar!"

"Holy hell Molly, what shows have you been watching?" Jonny says taking the spoon from me. "No one says that!"

"So, what do they say then?"

Jonny holds the spoon up and moves to speak. I hold my breath, *go on Jonny, do it! You can do it! Please sing, please let it out, come on...* For a moment I am sure he's in the zone, that the rock star inside of him is ready to come out. I bite my lip. Jonny pales and throws the spoon down onto the counter.

"So what delights are you creating?" He asks eventually, his voice catching in his throat.

I attempt jovial but it just sounds fake. "Well, I'm going for a roasted veg, pasta dish with a side of profiteroles!"

"Sounds good."

"Jonny..."

"Don't, Molly, I know what you're going to say, please don't."

"What's a crocodile's favourite game?" I ask him the only joke I know.

"I don't know!"

"Snap!"

Jonny smiles. "That's terrible!"

"Ok, you do better!" The challenge is set, and he raises an eyebrow at me.

"Fine! What do you call a man with a bird on his head?"

"Dunno!" I reply.

"Cliff."

"Oh my god!" I groan and shake my head, "that was worse than my joke!"

"It definitely wasn't! Your talent for snakes and ladders I'll agree on, but joke telling, that's a no from me!"

"Hmmm, slating my singing and my joke telling, it's just as well I'm good at my job otherwise I'd be a complete waste of space!"

"What do you love most about your business?" Jonny asks.

I chew on my lip while I think. "Is it a cop out to say all of it? It's so varied, one minute I'm sanding down a vintage wardrobe to repaint it, the next I'm in a smart suit, on a train to London to chat about colour schemes or I'm working on an interior design qualification, because some people won't hire me unless I have letters after my name. No day is the same and I love it. I just love what I do. I can't imagine ever going back to accounts."

"You should see what you could do with this place." Jonny says, liberally adding pasta to the pan of boiling water. "When you can actually see it!"

"This hotel has a vibe, Jonny. I can't quite explain it particularly while it smells of damp, but there is a magic here."

"Magic? No definitely not! There's no magic here, it's just a bad, bad mistake."

"I think you're looking at it all the wrong way because you had no choice but to move here. Maybe it feels like a mistake because you have something to bear the brunt of how unhappy you are, it's a physical thing that you can hate." I shake my head, "maybe I'm romanticising it because I see it as the place that gave me sanctuary when I needed it. In normal light, perhaps it is a shit hole but

173

don't believe that. I think it could be a huge money maker for you."

"How so?"

"You've got a prime location, all these cosy rooms, a chef who can make the best puddings, the swimming pool is in a chapel...When you look at all the pluses it's completely fabulous. Also, the advantage to the storm causing so much damage is that you could give it a complete refurb on the insurance! This building *is* a sanctuary, Jonny and that's what people need. Honestly, you could make a fortune!"

"Could I afford your fees though?"

"My fees?"

"Supposing I did redo it all and turn it into a sanctuary, I wouldn't want anyone else to create that. The job would be yours."

"Really? I'll give you mates rates! Although, you've not seen anything I've done, so you may not like my style."

"You may not like this hotel."

"True, but it's saved me so what's not to love? Plus, a massive job like this would save my most pressing issue!"

"Which is?"

"I'm going to have move out of my flat and decent one-beds in Bath are really expensive to rent. At least this would be a live in job, being so far away from home." My eyes sting and a single tear rolls down my cheek. "Damn it, I'm not supposed to cry."

Jonny wraps his arms around me. "Just let it out, Molly."

I nestle into his firm chest and wrap my arms around his neck. He rests his head on my shoulder and we softly sway to the music. In this moment I feel complete, and that is the scariest feeling of all.

Jonny

Molly has gone to my office to continue her search for my missing millions, so I do another leak-tour of the building. I think about Molly has said, and as I walk around, I try to see it through her eyes. I'm surprised to find that I don't hate it as much as I did a couple of days ago. I think she may be right, it just needs some love and attention. The hotel is a bricks and mortar version of me. Maybe this rash and drunken purchase has opened up more opportunities than it has taken away, despite my mindset over the past five years. *It's given you Molly.* Yeah, I don't want to think about that. I don't want to think about how my heart did a little skip when she said she couldn't go back to the flat she shares with Paul.

I hate that she's worrying about renting a flat. I hate that her boyfriend is a total tosser, she deserves so much better than that. I hate that I can't wrap her up and keep her here, but I'm no good for her. I'm toxic. Any one of the women who have been in my life would say the same. *But, you've never met anyone like Molly before.*

I don't understand what Molly see that the others didn't. Why does she tell me that it's not my fault? How can it not be? I've shit all over people my entire life, but Molly seems to think I'm better than I think I am. I just know that she will only end up realising what everyone else already knows.

You nearly sang in the kitchen. I felt something. It was deep inside, but it was there, a tiny vibration that pulsed in my belly. So tiny that I could have missed it, but in that split second between taking the spoon and putting it down, I felt it.

"Holy fuck." I sit down on one of the beds in the room I'm checking. "Holy fucking fuck." Then I cry. Not a snotty, dribbly cry but a silent release of much that has

175

been pent up over the years. I've held onto the belief that my dad was right, that I was nothing more than a *fucking kid who deserves a fucking beating,* so I did everything I could to prove him right. I was never going to be him, but somehow, I ended up as pointless as he is. Except now there is something else bubbling under the surface, and that is the flicker of hope that Molly may be right.

"Jonny?" I can hear her calling me from the staircase. "Jonny? Jonny? JONNY?"

I wipe my face on the hem of my tee-shirt and rush out of the room. She's standing on the bottom steps hollering at me.

"What's the matter? Don't tell me something else has broken?"

"Oh my God, man, I've been yelling for ages. I've literally been all over looking for you, I'm surprised you've not heard me! No, nothing has broken but fuck, Jonny. Come down, in fact, come to the bar…"

"But the hotel…"

"Fuck the leaks, come down."

"Why?"

"Because I need a bloody drink and you will too. Will you please come down."

Shit. What now?

I follow her down the staircase, across the damp reception floor and into the bar. There is an overpowering smell of wet wool from the lounge, and I pull a face. "That smell is revolting."

"It really is." Molly goes behind the bar and flashes the torch at the bottles on the shelf. Finding what she wants she gets two glasses from underneath and liberally pours the alcohol into both.

"Molly?"

"Yes?"

"What is that?"

"Probably your most expensive brandy."

"Why? What the fuck has happened?"

She comes to sit down on the sofa opposite me and puts the two glasses down on the table. From the pocket of the joggers she pulls out several sheets of folded paper.

"This has happened."

"Please don't tell me I'm not insured for flood damage."

Molly blows air from her mouth loudly and then speaks slowly. "It's nothing to do with the flood, it's to do with your money. Jonny, what do you know about GameNeekz?"

"Who?"

"GameNeekz." She repeats.

"Never heard of them."

"Really? They are a gaming company. They started in someone's bedroom, and I think they are probably still there!" She shakes her head. "So, if you don't know who they are then I assume you didn't know you have a certificate dating back to nineteen-ninety-five that shows you invested a hundred grand in the company?"

"How much? What a waste of money! It's no wonder I'm skint."

She gives me a sharp look. "Well, as it turns out, it really wasn't a waste. Your share is now worth..." She looks down at one of the papers, "about half the company value according to this certificate. From the looks of things, you gave them the entire amount needed to grow the business in exchange for half the company!" She shakes her head, "and you have no idea! How much money did you have that meant you could forget shit like this?"

"Too much! To be fair, I was probably drunk when I handed over the cash!"

Molly pulls a face, "is that your excuse for everything?"

I shrug. "Pretty much!"

"Hmm," Molly says looking unimpressed, "well, you have a big stack of post from them shoved into a box that you've never opened!"

"I probably just assumed they were bills, most of my post is."

Molly nods. "So it seems! There are masses of unopened envelopes in boxes in your office. I don't know how you can ignore them all, it would give me sleepless nights."

"Did you call me down to talk to me about my post?"

"No," she says crossly, "I've called you down because although GameNeekz is still a small business size-wise, in terms of games and gamers they are huge. Like, monumentally huge. They released one game last year that went to the top of the gaming charts and stayed there for months and months. They've won awards and everything!"

"I didn't have you down as a gamer!"

"I bloody hate games consoles. I only know about this company because Paul has all their games and had to go on the waiting list to get the most recent one! He's addicted! There are fan sites dedicated to their games! Honestly, these people are total nerds. Your share is going to be worth...and this is just a guess, but millions I reckon because the owners definitely are millionaires, despite them being complete geeks, so if they are then you are too! It's highly likely that the post is because they have been trying to pay you profits as per the certificate!" She shakes her head slowly, "I need a drink!"

"Millions?"

"Give or take. I'm not exactly sure because I haven't opened any of the post. But, holy moly, your current situation should never have happened, because you had that investment! I think you should open all the envelopes and see what the letters say!" She picks up her brandy and takes a long drink, before coughing. "Yuck, brandy is like bad medicine. But that's not all."

"No?" My head is reeling. Millions? I've been living in misery for all this time with access to money I've no idea about. Fuck. "What else have I got that I've forgotten I had?"

"Well, while I was rummaging in a box trying to find answers to the GameNeekz shares I found a solicitor's letter," she waves it at me, "that shows you own a castle on a Scottish island somewhere. Again, I can't find out anything about it because I can't get online. It was bought in nineteen-ninety-four in the name of John Jones. Is that you?

"It was, a long time ago."

"Well, that explains why you still have it rather than sell it when you sold everything else. It wasn't listed in your current name. A fucking castle! How posh is that? I wonder if you have a title to go with it. Lord Jonny of Rock Star or something!" She laughs before she says. "Did you know about it?"

"A castle?"

"Yes, as in a proper castle that belonged to a king once. Well, I assume so, who else would have owned a castle on a Scottish island other than a king. Or a queen!"

"Oh."

"Oh? OH? Is that all you can say?"

"I don't know what to say, I'm in shock!"

"Me too, and it's not my cash! You really did have too much money!" Molly picks up her glass. "I'm scared as to what else I will find buried in your office! I mean, what has your accountant been doing..."

"Paying debts mostly."

"Well, I have to be honest, Jonny, you really need to sack him because he should have known about all of this. I know the firm that he is partner of, and they are really expensive. It looks to me like he's being doing fuck all to earn his payments from you. If I could find this in some boxes, he should have been able to find your money by now. He's been taking the piss!"

"He's probably just washed his hands of me or, he's waiting for me to be in a fucking reality show so I can pay his bill."

"At least you won't have to do that now!"

"Hmmm." I'm not sure I have the right words to say anything. I can't fucking believe it. Millions, possibly, in a tech company I've never heard of. A castle in Scotland. What the fuck? None of this is making any sense but it's all there in black and white. I wonder if Freddie knew I'd spent this money, he usually oversaw all my outgoings, sending information to the accountant. I don't know whether to ring and ask him, but the last conversation didn't go very well and I'm still feeling raw about it.

"Jonny? You've gone really pale."

"You know, Molly. I've been totally skint for the past five years, and because of that I've lost more-or-less everyone I thought mattered, because they all had an agenda, and I had no idea. The less I could give them, the less they gave a fuck about me, and I was so wrapped up in my failure I didn't notice. My manager, Freddie, was my closest friend, or so I thought, but a few days ago he proved that it was all down to what I could pay him, and nothing to do with being my friend. That really fucking hurt. After twenty-five years of paying him ten percent, he just calls me to say, do the reality show or cheerio. I've been a fucking idiot and until you showed up, I had no idea how much of an idiot I've been."

"I don't think you're an idiot…"

"I have been." I screw up my face. "Your being here has opened my eyes."

"It has? To what?"

"To how empty my life has been empty. Apart from Aria, obviously. Everyone has wanted something from me, and I didn't realise what a toll that has taken to not be able to give them what they want." I feel a gut-wrenching pain and my head flops into my hands. "I think I was just too grateful to have the *yes* people around, because then I wasn't the *fucking little shit who should never have been born.* Being Jonny Raven didn't help me escape, it helped me buy affection."

"What about Chelsea?"

"She is just the same as all the others. She wanted my name, my fame, all of it. She never just wanted me. Aria's mum is decent, but I didn't treat her right, because she just wanted me to be a husband when I just wanted to be a rock star. Susie aside, I think I chased people who didn't give a shit because when I was little all I wanted was for my dad to give a shit."

"Jonny…"

"You have changed everything. You make me feel as though there is something good about to happen, and it's fucking terrifying." I drain the glass of brandy in one and screw up my face.

"Jonny? Are you ok?" Molly is looking anxiously at me and for a moment there is total silence as we just hold each other's gaze and I feel a tightness in my chest. There will be a massive hole in my life when she leaves.

I shake my head. "No, I don't think I am. I'm going to go for a swim. I need to think."

Molly looks surprised but doesn't say anything, just sits staring down at her glass of brandy. I leave the room quickly, knowing if I stayed for a moment longer, I would take her in my arms and the line I'm fighting to stay the right side of, would be crossed. She has saved my life, but by me opening the door to her, I've literally screwed hers and now I've left her looking nervous and uncomfortable. The leaks have been forgotten as I rush along the corridor towards the chapel, only the torch for light. Perhaps swimming in the dark isn't my greatest idea but it puts space between us and more importantly, it keeps me away from the whiskey and a whiskey would be ideal right about now.

The wind whistles through the gaps in the arched windows but the sky has lightened further. The rain isn't coming down in the same thick sheets as before and the outside world doesn't look as malevolent. The storm is blowing itself out which means the clock is ticking on Molly being here. Then what? I guess I face the truth. Chelsea and I need to divorce, I can pay her a settlement, if what Molly said about the tech firm is true. She can be free to live the celeb life she wants in London, and forget she was ever married to me. She forgets most days anyway, at least there will no longer be anything to tie her here.

What about you? There will be some money, it'll take the pressure off. Maybe rehab again for therapy, to sort my shit and let go of the past. Maybe I'll finally get my music back or maybe I'll go and live in the castle and keep the fuck away from anyone I could possibly hurt. Who the fuck knows what my future holds. I want to sing again. I want to open my mouth and not be fucking terrified that nothing will come out. I want to break the hold my deadbeat father has had over my life, and I want to find my mum. I need to know if she is alive, and why she went back. He said that I have siblings – are they like him? Are they like me? Would it make me feel whole if I knew?

I push open the chapel door. The rain patters on the tiles but it's less forceful than it was. I rip off my tee-shirt and shorts and jump into the navy water. The coldness takes my breath away but as I start to swim my mind goes quiet and I pull myself through the water, focusing on the stroke, the kick, the breath and I leave the thoughts behind until there is silence.

Molly

I sit watching as the logs in the wood burner spark and crackle. It's hypnotic. There are patterns in the dancing flames and the yellows and oranges of the fire feel so warm. My brandy is discarded on the table and alongside it is a glass of water. I have a headache and the water is meant to help, but it doesn't. I don't think there is a cure for this. It's the noisy, overcrowded thoughts that are causing my head to hurt and with Jonny out of the room, there is nothing to distract from them.

I sigh. It's getting harder to convince myself I'm not *that* person because I want to be. I'm swinging so fast between morally right and morally wrong that I'm going dizzy. It all started with the picture from the magazine, and the inexplicable pull to a man I'd never heard of. Fate throws the strangest curve balls at times. If this happened because I'm meant to leave Paul and change my path then it's succeeded, there isn't any going backwards, but that aside, I don't know what the universe is trying to tell me. I just know what I am trying to ignore, and that is the overwhelming and unnerving feelings I'm having about my host.

Why is it so much easier to think about leaving Paul than it is to think about leaving here?

How fucked up is that?

I can't sit here obsessing because it's driving me crazy, so I drink the water down and wrap the blanket around my shoulders. I give the fire a prod and pick up my torch, leaving the safety of the bar to do a leak check. I walk up the few steps to the lounge, which smells even worse than earlier. The water has puffed up the wool carpet, and it squelches under my feet, but at least the beautiful grand piano's legs don't look to have swollen from the wet. I feel strangely relieved about that. I don't try to open the door to the conservatory but the towels down on the floor haven't got any damper, so I'm hopeful that the storm is continuing to subside. It doesn't sound as loud now, and the sky has turned more lilac than it was earlier. The wind still howls but the roars of the sea are further away. I wonder if my car is still upside down against the break wall. That horrific experience seems so long ago and now the only thing that terrifies me is walking out the door and never seeing Jonny again.

I check the windows and stare out at a world that looks so different. The landscape is desolate, trees have fallen down, or are missing their leaves and flowers have lost their heads. It's still raining but the pitter patter on the window panes doesn't sound as frightening now. It's all changing. Nothing stays the same. The time I have left here is borrowed, the clock is ticking and then I will leave.

Shit.

Real life is waiting for me but I'm not ready, not at all.

I wander around the hotel. The light coming in from the windows makes checking for leaks so much easier, but I find myself getting more and more distracted by the building. Damp and water damage aside it is far more fabulous than I'd realised. It's retained most of its original features with fireplaces in bedrooms and carved ceiling roses above every light fitting. I'd not noticed in the dark just how spectacular the hotel was, despite the bad wallpaper and dated, pattered carpets. If Jonny's insurance pays out for all the damage, he could make this property something so special that people will be queuing for rooms.

I feel a frisson of excitement in my belly. To be a part of the renovations would be a dream come true for a new interior designer like me, *it would also bring you back to*

Jonny. And there lies the problem. "Arse." I mutter, wiping down the window with a towel. "Big, fat arse."

"I hope you're not talking about my arse?" Jonny says lightly behind me. Even his voice is enough to flip my stomach upside down.

"Nope, I was just thinking about life outside the hotel." Liar, liar pants on fire.

"You'll be back to life outside soon enough! The weather has got better. There is something to see outside even if it's just destruction and debris, but that's less isolating than the dark grey."

"Hmm." I reply, sitting down on the bed. "I was wondering if my car is still upside down on the road, or if it's at the bottom of the sea."

"If it is still there it's probably not driveable. Do you have breakdown cover?"

I nod. "Can you imagine the conversation? *Hello, I need a tow-truck to take me back to Bath, only my car is upside down and mangled against a sea wall. What happened dear? Well, tow-truck lady, the sea had a bad day and trashed my car!*" Jonny laughs and I grin. "It just sounds so far-fetched doesn't it!"

"The truth is stranger than fiction."

"It really is! How was your swim?"

"It was good. I needed to clear my head, there was just too much to take in – castles and money and realisation, although I'm hungry now! I'm heading down to the kitchen. Coming?"

"Sure."

I stand up and smooth the bedspread out. "I've had a good look around and the hotel has so much potential, Jonny. I had no idea that it was filled with so many treasures, until now."

"Treasures? It's filled with shit, revolting wallpaper and hideous carpets." Jonny says, running his hands

186

down the wall. "I mean, who chooses bottle green stripes?"

"Imagine it cream, with gold painted ceiling roses and rich red sofas and bedding. Gorgeous bold paintings on the walls and a bone china tea service…"

"Bone china?"

"Yes, there are loads of fab china items in charity shops that would cost you barely anything but would make a real impact and be in keeping with the building. I mean, these are great," I pick up some unimaginative cups, "but too similar to a chain hotel. You want quirky, timeless, luxury. Honestly, the more I see, the more I am convinced that this could make you a fortune."

"It may be more hassle than it's worth." Jonny walks across the room and holds open the door. "Although, if I do have some cash, and you want a big project, then knock yourself out!"

"It just needs some love, Jonny."

"Don't we all," he mutters. I think he meant for it to be under his breath, but I caught every sad syllable, and my chest tightens. He's more amazing than he realises, and I feel a pang that he has been through so much and still lost everything. He says it's karma, but maybe he's just a victim of his past because all I can see is a good person. He's kind, self-depreciating and so insanely handsome he could almost not be real. I feel better around him but maybe that's not real either. Maybe none of this is. Maybe I banged my head in the storm and I'm in a coma somewhere. I groan. Why am I trying to justify everything, like there is something to justify? Nothing has happened. We have behaved, we have been nothing more than friends thrown together by chance and regardless of the looks and the feelings that are simmering away, nothing will happen. Even if I would sell my soul to the devil just to be able to kiss him.

"That was a groany groan!" Jonny says lightly, "something wrong?"

"No, not really." I reply. "Just thinking."

"Thinking is overrated," he says, casually leaning his arm around my shoulder as we walk down the staircase. I'm not sure I breathe. He smells so good. Too good. It takes all my willpower not to wrap mine around his waist, because I want to. Oh, how I want to. "What are you hungry for?"

Oh God, don't ask me that.

"Just a snack of some sort." I say, "I can't justify another huge meal after all that pasta!"

"What else is there to do other than eat and check for leaks?"

Oh God, don't ask me that either.

"We could play snakes and ladders!" I say giggling.

"I don't plan on flattering your champion ego today!" Jonny laughs. We turn at the bottom of the stairs and take the staff route to the kitchen. The shrill whistles of the wind through the small windows have quietened considerably, but in my head the clock ticks louder. Time is running out.

The kitchen is cold, but we no longer need torches to see and the bucket under the drip is barely full. Jonny rummages in the fridge and calls out snack suggestions to me just as the lights begin to buzz and flicker then kitchen is suddenly flooded with a stark white. The electricity is back on.

"Thank fuck for that!" Jonny says using his hand to shield his eyes from the light.

I catch a glimpse of myself in the polished steel. "Or not! What a mess!" My hair is stuck up all over the place and I'm sure I have remnants of makeup on my face, despite washing it daily. I look like something the sea threw up and standing opposite Jonny who looks rugged and rock-star-y I feel horrific. "Maybe things were better with the lights off!"

"Nah, nothing is better with the lights off!" Jonny says grinning. He wets the edge of a tea-towel and uses it to carefully rub mascara away from under my eye. He's too close. Waaaaay to close. His hand is soft on my face, and I don't dare look up into the silver pools. I don't trust myself. "There you go! Perfect!"

"I wish!"

"If only you could see what I do."

"I could say the same about you."

Jonny sighs, "maybe it's good that we don't think about it, hey?"

"Maybe it is." I turn from him and catch my breath. "This kitchen is even more fabulous in the light. It's huge!" I don't give a shit about the size of his kitchen. I just need to make conversation so I don't throw myself at him. Shit, shit, shit. SHIT.

In the full light Jonny is spectacular. Older than the photo I kept from the magazine, and more world-weary and tired, probably from the strange hours we've been keeping, but I have never seen a more god-like looking man ever. His hair is chestnut with the odd smattering of grey around the temples, and across his jaw is days-old growth that seems to frame the full lips. God, he's so hot, I'm practically drooling, which is not a good look on me. I'm so conscious of how I look compared to him, slightly too chubby, with hair that hasn't been brushed since the morning of the storm. I am certain he knows that I'm taking my time looking at the kitchen, so I don't have to look at him.

"It's a good kitchen." There is humour in his voice. "Are you always this enthusiastic about kitchens.

Shit, he definitely knows!

"Yep," I lie blithely, "it's my job!"

"You're full of crap, Molly, you're just worried about what you look like in bright lights!"

He has me figured! "Well, so would you be."

"I couldn't give a shit."

"That's because you look like you!" I mutter.

"What? An old, broke, forgotten, has-been, drunk? That's hardly 'sexiest man of the year' material!"

"Did you win sexiest man of the year?" I ask, sniggering.

"I sure did, five times! Then I was beaten by some boy bander! You would have fancied him! He was right up your street with his neatly combed hair and cheeky boy-band grin!"

"Damn it! I've never won anything other than snakes and ladders! You're way cooler than me."

"Well, duh!" Jonny says laughing. I throw a forgotten tomato at him which bursts on his face. "You're so dead," he growls and scoops me up, running through the hotel with me squirming in his arms, and launching me into the pool.

"Oh my god, you shit!" I splutter as I reach the surface. Clambering out of the water I pull at his waist, but he's too strong for me and I end up in the water again. "I am going to get you for this! I am going to sing every minute of every hour until the rain stops."

"Oh, fuck!"

"You've done it now," and I launch into the loudest tuneless version of a pop song until he clasps his hands over his ears.

"If I let you throw me in, will you stop?"

"I'll stop if you get me a towel, a coffee and a big pile of profiteroles!"

"Deal!"

Jonny

"I think you should open these." Molly says coming into the bar with a box of post and dumping it on the floor in front of me. On top of the box is her phone.

"Do you want to charge that?"

"I think I should, people may be worried."

"Paul?"

She shrugs. "Maybe, but unlikely. I was more thinking about my parents and Ella."

"Ella?"

"My best friend. We normally talk every day. She'll be thinking I've died or something. Do you have a charger?"

"On the shelf under the till."

She collects it and leaves the room. I sigh. My phone is still on the small table, perhaps I should face real life too. I pick it up and walk upstairs to my suite, unlocking the door and pushing it open. Considering the amount of time that I ordinarily spend in my room, it now feels claustrophobic. After the freedom of wandering around the hotel, I'm not sure I can lock myself away with whiskey for company again. I sit down on the sofa and plug the charger into the phone. Here goes nothing.

The phone takes a while but then comes to life, beeping with messages from Aria along the lines of *Dad, I've seen the weather on news. Are you safe?* One message from Susie, one from Mr Cooper, the hotel GM but surprise, surprise nothing from Chelsea. I find I don't mind. I message Aria back and fling the phone onto a chair.

"Jonny?" Molly taps on the door and pushes it open. "Can I come in?"

"Sure."

"This is nice," she says looking around. "Tidy too, I'm so messy that I'm envious of tidy people."

"It wasn't tidy. A couple of days ago there was shit everywhere, I was living in a scum hole."

"Really?"

"Really. Things were bad, Molly, I couldn't even remember when I had last showered."

"Nice!" She laughs and then her face falls. "Jonny, I had a phone call."

"Who from?" I wonder why she tells me until her reply comes.

"Your wife."

I sit up. "Fuck."

"That covered half the conversation," she mutters. "Something along the lines of *why the fuck are you there with my fucking husband.* She was delightful."

"I'm so sorry. I left her a voicemail from your phone..."

"Perhaps you'd better call her." She sits down on the chair. "I looked at her Instagram," colour flushes across her cheeks, "I was intrigued but it's no wonder you feel shit, I would be devastated if Paul behaved like that."

"She's not all bad, Molly. She is a victim of my shit as much as I am. She just needs to be someone, and she doesn't have the ability to deal with my stuff. She's needy, her self-esteem is linked to being known, and she doesn't have that with me."

"It sounds exhausting."

"She is!" I look down at my phone. "I guess I'll call her."

"I'll leave you to it."

"Did Paul call you?"

"No, just a couple of texts. Twat." She stands up and puts her phone in the pocket of the joggers. "Ella says I can go and stay with her for a while, which may help initially. Goddamn it." She leaves the suite, slamming the door behind her. My instinct is to go after her, except I don't. I call Chelsea.

"Who the fuck was that I spoke to?" She screeches down the phone at me, without pausing for breath. "Why the fuck are you all alone with another woman? Have you been screwing her? I mean, you never want to fucking screw me…"

I take a deep breath in. "Chelsea…"

"Don't fucking *Chelsea* me, when you've been fucking someone else."

"I haven't fucked anyone…"

"So, who the fuck is she?"

"She got caught in the storm, nearly died and ended up here." I say, leaning back and closing my eyes. *She is also the most incredible person I've ever met, and I don't want her to leave.* "She's staying until the weather changes."

"Oh, right, whatever. Anyway, don't forget the party is next week." Chelsea's ability to change the subject never ceases to amaze me.

"What party?"

"For fuck's sake, Jonny, do you not listen to anything I say? We're having a party, everyone is coming, it's next Saturday."

"Chelsea, the hotel has been flooded, there isn't going to be a party."

"So, clear it up. That's what you have staff for."

"It will take more than staff…"

"It can't be that bad, it was just a bit of rain!" I know she's not listening. "Make sure the bar is full. I've got to go. I'm meeting Indigo for cocktails." Her phone clicks off without even a goodbye. Yes, my decision to end my marriage is the right one.

A party? Who is she kidding?

∗∗∗

Molly has a glass of red wine in front of her and she's scrolling through her phone when I get back to the bar. She looks tense and the atmosphere in the room feels awkward.

"Is there much going on in the world?" I ask, breaking the silence.

"Just emails and a few furniture enquiries. I'm trying to reply to them, but it feels like an effort. Besides," she rolls onto her side and picks up the glass, "how can I talk about furniture when I have no idea where I'll be living. In an ideal world Paul will move out, but I know it will be me. It sucks, I love the flat."

"You haven't changed your mind then?"

"Nope. He sent a couple of texts asking if I was alright. Not one voicemail. Not one. That's not how you treat someone you love. It's made my decision easier." She takes a long drink of her wine. "Fuck it, Jonny. Fuck. It."

"That's fighting talk!"

"I know! Grrrr! She laughs. "I feel weird that life is returning to normal. I liked being shut away, even if I had to nearly die to have it. Being back online just feels busy and chaotic, it's much easier to live in the dark and eat pudding!"

"The profiteroles need eating up."

"I think I'll puke if I eat anymore! I definitely need carbs. I'll never be thin! Your wife is thin…"

"Yes, she is." There is no point avoiding the comments. "She exercises a lot, parties a lot and doesn't eat a lot. She used to be softer, but it changed when her friends changed."

194

"Well," she holds up an Instagram photo of Chelsea, "she looks good."

"Most of it is surgery."

"Oh."

"Don't compare yourself to women on Instagram, Molly. It's not real."

"I know," she sighs, "but when you're feeling low, it's hard not to."

"Do you want to talk about it?"

"No, being here is enough."

She pours me a glass of wine and hands it to me. Our hands touch and neither of us move. She looks at me, I look at her and everything else just fades away.

Molly

Somehow, we managed to forget the complexities of the life waiting for us outside of the storm. The red wine helped. So did the games of Cluedo. Jonny refused to play snakes and ladders for fear of losing but Cluedo was fun. We laughed. A lot. It was easy to pretend that Paul and Chelsea didn't exist in the midst of the laughter, and in the stillness between words. We were safe in those moments, choices didn't have to be made, reality didn't have to be faced, the unknown future didn't have to be considered. If our hands touched, we didn't rush to move them, nor did we hurry to turn our gaze away if our eyes met. We were crossing the line, slowly, and had Jonny not made an excuse to leave the bar, I think we would have stepped over it.

I don't want to be a cheater, but despite nothing physical happening, my feelings are at odds with my morals. It makes me feel bad.

I wander around the hotel, exploring rooms I've not seen. There are small, intimate rooms everywhere, but when I reach the library, I stop exploring. It's the most beautiful room. It has floor-to-ceiling shelves crammed with books and at each end are huge fireplaces. The windows are arched and clear, except at the top where there are patterns made from coloured glass. I can't see the view as day has turned to the navy blue of night, but I sit down on the chaise longue and wonder what it looks like in here when the sun is high. I like it in here, I could lose myself in this room.

"There you are!" Jonny comes into the library. "I've been looking all over for you."

"Why?"

"I was going to make some dinner! You've been missing for ages!"

"Have I? I've been in here. I love this room. It feels so inspiring. Maybe it's the smell of the books…"

"Or the smell of the damp running down the wall."

I give him a look. "Where's your imagination?"

"In the damp running down the wall!"

"The hotel just gets more perfect for a retreat with each room I see! All the little snug areas and all the character, even if it's under the bad décor. I love it here Jonny. It's going to be hard to leave."

Shit. I didn't mean to say that.

"What? This manky old building?"

"Yep." We both know what I meant, but I'm grateful that he kindly saved my blushes. "Is this a door behind the panelling?"

"Yes, but don't open that…"

It's too late, I pulled the door open before he could finish asking me not to. It's a small walk-in cupboard with a light pull and, when I turn the light on, the gold that glints at me is blinding.

"Oh my God, are these all yours?" The cupboard is full of framed discs and awards haphazardly dumped on the floor. I pick one up, "I'd like to thank you for this award…" I giggle, "why are these shoved in a cupboard? They should be pride of place."

"Please shut the door." Jonny's face has gone pale, and he looks as though I've uncovered his most shameful secret.

"But…"

"Shut the fucking door."

His voice breaks and the sound is so raw that I drop the award I am holding. "Jonny."

He shakes his head. "Please don't say anything, please just shut the door."

I step out of the cupboard and close the door behind me. Jonny clenches and unclenches his fists like he's battling with something, and I take his hands in mine. "You hide these things away," I say gently, "but all it does is make you afraid. You have every right to be proud of those awards, so few people ever achieve what you have, but you have given your power away and you need to claim it back. When we were dancing, I could feel the music inside you. It wants to come out. It is who you are."

"Not anymore."

"You are not your father, Jonny."

"I need a drink." He wrenches his hands from mine and leaves the library, slamming the door so hard it bounces back on its hinges. I just let him go. The conflict between what I said and what he believes was raging in his eyes. I know it's all in there, he just has to let it out. The trouble is, we believe what we tell ourselves and rewriting it is the hardest challenge of all.

Jonny

I slam the bottle down on the kitchen worktop and stare at it. It's the answer to the mindless nothingness that I need and the quietening of the voices that tell me I'm worthless on repeat. It's the answer to everything. Except it's not. No amount of whiskey will dull this ache. The burn as it slides down my throat won't put out the fire of conflict that rages inside of me. It will make everything worse. *It may make things better.* No, it won't. It promises a numbness, a nothingness, to shut out all the shit that my life has become and wrap me up in its warmth. It would be easy. To drink until I feel nothing, to forget about my waster old man, or the waster that I've become. I was never going to be this person. Never. To be comparable to my father makes me sick to my stomach and rage erupts from me, until I'm smashing pans down on the counter tops and roaring like an anger-monster from the depths of hell. Because that's where I am. In hell. A hell of my own making because I'm a fucking idiot. My father's son. The person I vowed I would never, ever be. I'm it. I'm him.

I clench my hands into fists and ball them against my eyes. I need to shut out the pain, the ripping and tearing as the mass grows and grows, taking my breath and pushing it from my body until I can't get any air in. The darkness comes for me, groaning and wailing, its terrifying grip getting tighter and tighter. My father speaks from the blackness – words from so long ago, words that should mean nothing now, but mean everything because I am him. I am the man I hate. I deserved to lose my music. I deserve to have nothing. I am no better than the man who broke me into pieces and left my mother dying. The pain in my chest is crushing me, sucking my life from me. I can hear anguish, the animal sound in the air and I know that the anguish is mine. Something shatters and there is a scream, it's chilling, deathly and agonised and I'm sure I will die, until warmth wraps itself around me and holds me tightly, bringing me back.

Bringing me back to life.

"It's ok," the warmth whispers. "I've got you. It's ok."

Molly

Jonny is lying on the sofa, a blanket over him and he's staring into the flames. There is soft music piping through the speakers and a calmness in the room. It's cooled in here and the blanket that covers me isn't as snug as it was. My tired body wants to go to bed, but I'm fearful of the day ending, because I know that this is the last day. The storm has blown itself out and there is no more savage clattering of the elements against the building.

My gut twists and the heavy weight rests again on my chest. What will we become on the other side of this strange time? Will Jonny get some help, will he sing again? And me? Who am I outside of Paul and Molly? Who will I be when I can sing as loudly as I want and not have someone complain about it? *You will be you. Wholly, unapologetically, you.* I will go dancing with Ella, I will drink too many cocktails and laugh about nothing. I will stay in bed all day eating crisps, because no one will tell me I can't. I will make my own decisions and not worry that criticism will follow. I will grow and evolve and be the best version of me. I will be proud of my success and celebrate it. That's who I'll be.

I'll also be the girl who fell in love with a broken rock star.

Because I have. Completely.

I look over at Jonny. His profile is strong – the straight nose, the full lips, the masculine jaw – I will miss him every moment of every day. I wonder if he will miss me.

Jonny sighs.

"Are you ok?" I ask.

"I guess. I was just thinking about tomorrow and what it will be like when your bad singing isn't here anymore."

"You'll miss it!"

"Yeah, I will." My heart skips a beat. Jonny yawns. "I feel worn out though Molly. These are the first sober sleeps I've had in years. I think my body is as fucked as my mind."

"Do you want to go to bed?"

He grins cheekily. "Is that an invitation?"

"Jonny!"

He laughs. "You're so easy to shock!"

"I am not!"

"You are! It's because you're so sweet and lovely." He turns to face me. "Are you cold?"

"A little."

"Here," he says and holds back his blanket, "I'm hot!"

I giggle nervously and against my better judgement I leave the safety of my sofa, for the comfort of his.

Thursday

Jonny

What have I done? What have I done? What the fuck have I done?

I wake up with Molly curled up alongside me, her soft body warm and feminine. Lying with her like this is dangerous, but I can't make myself move and instead, I pull her closer. She gives a small sigh, and I look down on her. Her dark lashes lay against the shadows under her eyes and the pale skin has a flush where the heat from our bodies has made her warm. She's so pretty, I could look at her forever and it still wouldn't be long enough. I'm aware of a wetness on my cheeks that I need to wipe away but if I do, I'll have to let Molly go, and I can't bring myself to do that. I never want to let her go but while she has brought me back to life, she is the ultimate price that I have to pay. Karma kicked me down over and over again for the past five years but has stuck the final boot in sending Molly here. To have someone so special this close for the shortest time, and then have to watch her leave is the lesson that nothing else could teach me. She is everything and I am nothing.

I must inadvertently squeeze her too tightly because she stirs and slowly opens her eyes.

"Don't cry," she whispers in a sleepy voice, looking up at me and gently wiping my cheeks with her thumbs. "Don't cry anymore, you've given too many tears away." She shifts and reaches her arm around me, snuggling her face into my chest. "I've got you, Jonny. I've always got you."

Her eyes flutter shut, and she falls back to sleep, her arm loosening from its position around my neck. A sob catches in my throat and I hold her to me while the tears flow silently. When I wake, the fire has burned out but there is a brightness coming from the lounge. Gently I uncurl from around Molly and ease myself off the sofa, following the light. The storm has given way to a light blue sky and the sun is shining, its yellow rays resting on the piano. Is it a sign? It feels like it could be but that may just be wishful thinking. *You nearly sang in the kitchen.* The voice in my head is almost too loud to ignore. I walk towards the piano and lift the lid. This was the first brand new instrument I bought when I signed my record contract at eighteen. All my guitars had been from second hand shops, but the piano was my big prize. I paid cash because I'd finally made it.

I stroke my fingers over the keys, careful not to press them. They need a clean, some are sticky from spilled drinks and the sweat from other people's hands. Freddie thought I was insane for leaving it where anyone could bash out some notes and not give a shit about what the piano represented but by the time it was moved here, I didn't care. While guests played it, and slopped their cocktails over the polished maple, I hid in my suite with a bottle of whiskey for company.

Go on, Jonny. Play.

I sit down on the stool and look at the keys. My hands want to move but terror keeps them clenched in my lap. *Come on Jonny, one note.* I can hear the chords, smell the heat of the stadium, hear the cheers of the crowd but my eyes sting and the memories roll down my cheeks in a steady stream of tears. I never used to cry. It was a sign of weakness - *wipe your fucking face you snivelling little shit, or I'll give you something to cry about* – so I learned not to. Even when I was having beatings that made me see stars or watched as my dad rammed his fist into my mum, I didn't ever cry. I was too scared. So why has that fear left? *Molly.* I smash my hands down on the keys. What the fuck am I going to do without her?

"Jonny?" She stands on the steps looking at me, crumpled from sleep and looking anxious.

"I'm so sorry," I say, closing the lid. "I didn't think."

"No, it's ok, no need to be sorry, I just wanted to make sure that you're ok?"

"Yep, fine."

She scans my face, worry in her eyes. "You don't look fine."

"The sun is shining, everything is fine."

"Jonny, the sun shining doesn't make anything fine," she whispers. "Nothing is fine." Her phone rings from the bar and she turns from me to answer it. I can hear her from here, *Yes, Paul...no Paul...for fucks sake Paul the weather has only just changed...how do you think I'm going to get home, the car was turned upside down by the sea...BECAUSE I NEARLY FUCKING DIED IN IT...I will be home when I'm home...yes, I know it's stopped raining...BECAUSE I AM HERE...I can't do this now, I've got to figure it out...train probably...no I don't want to go out for tea...you can say sorry as much as you like, the fact is that YOU DIDN'T TELL ME...Stop asking me to calm down, you nearly drown and see how calm you feel...yeah, whatever, bye.*

I hear her mutter *prick* then she comes back up to the lounge.

"Yep, Jonny," she says sarcastically, "everything is really fine. I'm going for a swim, because otherwise I may lose my shit!"

She stomps off along the corridor towards the chapel and I take the opposite route to the library and slump down in a chair, my feet up on the small table. I look for what Molly sees, the intimacy, the comfort, the calmness but I just see emptiness. Today she will leave. There is no reason for her to stay and if I say nothing, she will go home and live her life far away from me. The best thing I can do for Molly is to let her go. I wish I'd not suggested that she got involved with any refurbishments on the hotel, but that is a problem easily solved. I hate that she may wait for my call. I hate that I will want to call. I hate that I will always wonder what happened to her. I hate that she will think I didn't care.

I blow a long breath out and stare out of the window while the minutes tick by. What a fucking mess. *It's a chance to have a clean slate.* Yeah, I suppose it is and maybe the clean slate I need is to face the past that I shut away in the cupboard. It was supposed to have been locked and the key thrown away, but someone missed that memo. *Go on Jonny, just one look.* I don't know what moves me from the chair, but my hand is suddenly on the door handle, and I'm opening the cupboard. I can't stop myself from turning on the light and looking down at the statues and framed discs. Proof that I'd made it. Proof that I wasn't always *a fucking waste of space that should never have been born* and proof that I'd been someone even if I can barely remember who that someone was.

I sit down on the floor, leaning against the wall and pick up an award. *Best Male Singer.* The next one *Best Album.* The next one *Artist of the Decade.* The next one *Sexiest Man Alive.* One by one I pick up the awards, dozens of them all telling the same story – I was a superstar once.

"Jonny?" Molly opens the door, her hair wet and a flush on her cheeks, "are you in here?"

"Yes, I'm down here!"

"What are you doing?"

"Having a trip down memory lane."

"Oh," she comes over and sits down beside me. "I was going to ask if you wanted some breakfast, but this looks more interesting." Molly smiles gently, "are you admiring your fabulousness?"

"I'm missing it." I pick up a framed platinum disc. "I'm not missing being the arsehole I was, but I'm missing this. It's a reminder that I did something right."

"Of course you did."

"You're so sure."

Molly shrugs, "we can all have regrets, Jonny. Some regrets are bigger than others. I regret that I stopped phoning Corey's mum and that I stopped going to his grave. That makes me an arsehole, but I can try to make up for it all. I can't take it away, but I can say sorry. You being an arsehole at times doesn't define you. I'm not sure you can say sorry to everyone woman you ever dumped, you probably can't remember most of them, but you'll find a way to make amends. Honestly, though, the person you need to say the biggest sorry to is yourself. I think you'll find your way back to all of this when you do. Carrying around all that self-loathing is going to take a toll, once you release it, you'll be -" she picks up an award, "- *Hottest Man in the Universe* again!" Molly laughs, "did they really give out these awards?"

Her laugh is infectious. "I did win awards for music too!" I say grinning.

"Come on Hot Man, let's get some food then we'll find somewhere to display these sexy man awards!"

"They are not being displayed anywhere!"

"When I do the refurb they will be!" She laughs, "they will be made into lamps and all sorts!"

"Maybe I need to rethink my choice of decorator." I say lightly although inwardly that's exactly what I'm thinking.

"Chicken!" She replies, holding out her hand to pull me up. "Come on, I'm starving!"

We walk down to the kitchen. It feels surreal to see everything in daylight.

"Do you want to walk down and check on your car?" I ask her as I push open the kitchen door. "If it's still on land then you can arrange a tow-truck."

"Are you trying to get rid of me?" She teases but there is a shadow over her face.

"Of course not!" I fill the kettle and switch it on.

"Hmmm!" Molly opens the fridge and wrinkles her nose. "Yuck, there is something very off in here, do you think we should clear out the fridges? Perhaps have cheesecake for breakfast?"

I open the second fridge. "Urgh, no thanks! Pancakes and syrup for me! Happy food! My foster mum, the lady who looked after me when we first moved north, made me pancakes for my first ever breakfast away from my dad, and since then they've been my favourite food. Before every show I'd have pancakes with maple syrup and it became a good luck talisman, or something."

"Did you stay in touch with your foster family?" Molly asks, picking out some questionable looking pastries from the fridge and chucking them in the big bin.

"No. I changed my name soon after I got my recording contract so they wouldn't have been able to find me anyway. I thought about having one of my team look for them, but I didn't want to answer any questions about my mum. I was too ashamed." I take the tray of eggs from the dairy fridge and put them on the counter top. Crossing the kitchen to the pantry I pick out flour and syrup. "Is there any milk that still smells alright?"

Molly opens a new bottle and sniffs. "This one is ok." She hands me the milk and I start measuring out the batter. "Can you believe you own a castle?" She adds spoons of coffee to the cafetiere. "I can't stop thinking about how cool it is."

"It is cool, and very bloody odd. Definitely not what I expected you to find buried in my office."

"Are you going to open your post?"

"Eventually."

"Today?"

"Yeah, maybe." I say, adding butter to the frying pan and turning up the heat. Molly watches me add the batter to the pan, chewing her lip.

"Are you scared to?"

"What?"

"Open your post?"

I ignore the question. Molly waits for me to flip the pancake before she speaks again.

"I think you are," she says, "I think you have gotten so used to thinking you have nothing that you don't know how to have something."

"Is that so?" I shake the pan and the pancake sizzles in the butter. Tipping it onto a plate I hand it to Molly. She adds a liberal coating of syrup and uses a fork to cut through the pancake. Popping a chunk into her mouth she chews thoughtfully.

"Yep, that is so!" Molly gestures to the pancake. "This is good. I never think to make them."

I busy myself making more. Molly pours the coffee and hands one to me, a fork hanging out of her mouth.

"I am scared," I admit, leaning against the work top to eat my breakfast. Molly raises an eyebrow. "Ok, you win, you're right! Suddenly there is the real possibility that I'm not skint anymore, and I don't know what that means."

"It means that you can't hide here being gloomy. It means that you have to go back out into the world."

"I'm not sure the world wants me."

"Actually, I think you will find that they do! I don't want this to freak you out, but I went onto my music app, and you are trending. That article has jogged people's memories."

"What? I'm trending? Fuck!" I feel the blood drain from my face. I've been so used to obscurity that I'm suddenly painfully unnerved.

Molly looks exasperated. "It's awesome, Jonny!" She says slowly, "it means that people are listening to your music, which means you will earn some money and you never know, you may win *Hottest Older Rock Star* at the next music awards!"

I throw a tee-towel at her. "You really do take the piss!"

"I know, it's part of my charm."

✳✳✳

"Ready?" I ask as we brace ourselves either side of the bookcase.

"As I'll ever be!" Molly grimaces, "it feels a little strange to be facing the brightness of the outside world after spending three days in the dark. I'm almost nervous and I have to be honest, still absolutely terrified about the sea." She hitches up the joggers I've loaned her. "I'm also a little scared that these will fall down as we're heaving the bookcase!"

Jonny laughs, "and in daylight too! Don't worry, if they do, I won't look!"

We start pulling the bookcase back and forth, scraping it across the tiles until it's leaning against the wall. The desk is harder to move, and I guess Molly must have been firing on adrenaline when the water poured in because it's awkward to move and heavier than I imagined. We leave it in the middle of the room, and I turn the key in the lock.

"The moment of truth," I say wryly.

The door needs a couple of hefty tugs to move. The wood has swelled after sitting in water and I have to yank it from its propped position and push it back and secure it into the wall hook. I'm not sure it will close again even if I manage to fix it back on the hinges.

I walk outside first then Molly follows hesitantly behind. The damage left by the storm is immense. Molly's face goes grey as she looks around at the landscape. Under the bright light of the sun, the destruction is as far as we can see. I can't imagine how much more the storm would have impacted the hotel if we'd been lower down. It would have been irreparable probably.

"Oh hell, just look at it all," Molly says, her eyes scanning the scene. "Armageddon has really struck."

"It's a fucking mess." The grass has been stripped away and, in its place, rolling down the hill are sludgy divots of mud. The slope is about four hundred metres from the road and sits on a forty-five-degree angle so for the water to come into reception means the waves were immense. I look at Molly whose bottom lip is wobbling as she stares at the ocean. I try to imagine the terror she must have felt in the middle of it, but I can't. I can't imagine it all. I wrap my arm around her shoulders, "come on Molly, let's go and see if your car survived."

"I'm not sure I can move."

"I've got you."

We skirt around debris, mud, fallen roof tiles and glass that litter the driveway and make our way slowly down to the gates. One of them has been knocked clean off its hinges and lies across the tarmac. We squeeze along the edge and down towards the sea road.

"The sea bridge is visible, that's a good sign," I tell her. Except it's not. It means that Molly can leave. I get a painful feeling in my gut.

"So is the rest of the peninsula, but look at the state of that," she says pointing down to the development kitchen.

212

The roof is missing, and the expensive glass frontage is smashed beyond repair. Next to it is a fine dining restaurant but there is little remaining of its front wall and the outdoor tables are nowhere to be seen.

"Thank god everyone got off away before the storm really hit," I say. I look back up the slope to the hotel. "We came off lightly in comparison." Molly stands beside the gateposts.

"I'm not sure I can go any further." She shivers.

The sea has retreated back behind the sea wall, but it still throws up huge frothy waves and crashes down forcefully. Molly's face is deathly pale.

"I've got you." I tell her, "I won't let anything happen to you."

"Promise?"

"Scouts honour."

She grips my hand tightly and takes a couple of steps. "I feel sick and I'm so cold I can't feel my hands." I take off my hoodie and hand it to her. She shrugs it on. "Thank you," she whispers, pulling the hood up over her head.

"The storm is over, Molly, you're safe. The sea won't come for you."

"How do you know."

"I just know."

She mutters to herself under her breath as we take slow steps along the sea road. Further down towards the development kitchen is her car crunched up against the sea wall and still on its roof.

"How the fuck did you get out of that?" I ask hoarsely.

"I don't know." Molly bursts into tears. "I just kicked and kicked the window until I could swim out." Her body shakes violently, and I wrap my arms around her, holding her as tight against me as I can. "The wave covered the

213

car, and I thought I was going to die. All I could think is that I was so alone, and I was going to die, and I was so scared that I wouldn't ever have the chance to really live, and really love and be the best version of myself. I hated Paul for me being here, but if I hadn't had come, I would never have met you. I don't want to leave, Jonny. I can't leave. Please ask me to stay."

"I can't," I choke, the lump in my throat constricting my breath. Her arms pull me closer and amongst the sobs I hear her say *oh*. It's a heart-breaking sound. My own tears roll down my face and fall onto the top of her head. I hold her so tightly trying to memorise how she feels in my arms. *What are you fucking doing, Jonny, ask her to stay* but the words won't come. I can't say them. *Don't let her walk out of your life, don't do it Jonny.* "I'm so sorry, Molly."

Molly

I don't want to let go because if I do then I'm letting go forever. The pain as my chest rips open is excruciating. He says that doesn't want me to stay but the weight of his arms around me and the tears I can feel dropping onto my skin tell me another story. This is the end, and he is breaking as much as I am. Our strange little world of two, safe together inside of a devastating storm, is over and my heart has shattered.

"I have to go," I whisper, squeezing my eyes shut. "I have to go now."

"Molly…"

The anguish in his voice is everything I need to know. I look up into his silver wolf eyes, and he looks down into my blue. His mouth parts and the tanned skin on his cheeks, flushes. I make a sound, a small one, a gasp perhaps and then his mouth is on mine. Everything is forgotten. The kiss is everything I ever wanted. There is an intensity in it that turns my insides to fire, and the hands on my face, burn where they touch my skin. I lose myself in his kiss, nothing outside of it exists. His palm moves from my face to my jaw and the other hand moves to the back of my head, holding me to him. I couldn't move, even if I wanted to. The need for him is too great, too powerful, too demanding. Finally, I feel whole. We fit. His mouth fits mine and mine fits his. We fit so completely that I feel sparks surround us. There is something outside of us holding this moment frozen in time, a moment that can't last, but for now, it is perfect. The one perfect moment.

Jonny is groaning softly against my mouth, a low sound that tells me exactly what he wants, and I want it to. I want Jonny so much I feel crazed by the feelings rushing through me. The kiss is overpowering, his hands on me have turned my skin to lava and my legs are barely holding me up. I've never wanted anyone so much.

"Molly," Jonny moans, "Molly, we have to stop."

"No." I whisper, pulling at his lower lip with my teeth.

Jonny pulls away from me and takes my wrists, standing back to make a space between us. "We have to stop." He says, his voice breaking.

"Why?" My voice cracks and I feel so much pain because his words are like a punch to the stomach.

He lets go of my wrists and rakes his hands through his hair, looking distraught. "Because you are worth so much more than this, worth so much more than me. Molly, I've told you how much I hurt people and I'm not going to do that to you."

"Well, Jonny, you just have."

I don't know how I find the strength to take a step backwards and turn away from him when every single part of me wants to stay. His rejection rips my insides out, but I make my way back up the slope towards the hotel, just about holding myself together. Tears flow steadily down my face, silent tears filled with such intense pain that they are acidic on my cheeks. He doesn't follow me.

The one perfect moment is over.

Jonny

Molly has gone.

A taxi collected her and now there is no sign that she was ever here, apart from the awards that still litter the floor in the library. I sit down beside them, the *Hottest Man in the Universe* award in my hand, but it's not funny anymore. A bottle of whiskey sits unopened on the library table where it has been since she left. She didn't say goodbye, but I watched from the window until the car went over the sea bridge. I thought whiskey would be the answer but there was a voice inside the anguish that told me I didn't want to drink to forget nor try and blot out the pain, because the pain means that she was here. I want to remember all of it, every single moment I spent with her - from the soaked waif that banged on the door to the beautiful woman who told me to believe in myself again. I have to stay sober because then Molly is real.

A door bangs and footsteps pad along the corridor. *Molly? Has she come back?* I hope so, fuck I hope so, I should never have let her go, what a fucking idiot.

The door swings open and I forget to breathe but the voice, when it comes, is all wrong.

"Hi honey, I'm home!"

To be continued in Electric Dreams,
coming 2023.

Author's Note

At times it didn't seem possible that I would ever get to the end but here we are, my eighth book, and I have to admit that saying goodbye to a story doesn't get any easier, no matter how many are written!

This book started as a dream about Jon Bon Jovi, randomly, about three years ago. In the dream it was dark, pouring with rain and for the duration of the dream there was a love affair that didn't go beyond a kiss that happened just as I woke up! From that dream, Jonny Raven was born and the location, well that was a lovely Cornish hotel that my family and I stayed in for a few nights one summer. It was a grey building that sat high on the cliff overlooking the sea. It rained then too, and although Jonny's hotel is more gothic, it clearly had an impact on me!

Molly's business was inspired by stories of women who lost their jobs during the covid lockdowns and created a new career for themselves out of those difficult times. If that was you, then please know you have been an inspiration, even if we have never met.

I could not have finished this book if it hadn't been for the amazing test readers who kept me going when my confidence waivered. Ladies, you are the best.

I am also so so so thankful to my family who don't seem to mind when I disappear into my own world and ignore them for weeks! My loves, despite me endlessly asking you to go away, I do love you!

And to you, THANK YOU for reading my book, let me know what you think!

Finally, to the people of Cornwall, thank you for lending my story your home – the negativity is a necessary part of the story and definitely not a reflection of my opinion of Cornwall, I think it is the most spectacularly beautiful county in England … just so you know!

So, on I go to Electric Dreams and the conclusion of Jonny and Molly's story. I hope it works out for them, but the real world is lying in wait, so it remains to be seen…

Love Katie xx

PS – typos are all mine!

Find me here
Website   katiejanenewman.co.uk
Insta   katiejanenewmanwriter
Facebook   Katie Jane Newman
Twitter   KJNewmanAuthor
TikTok   katienewmanwriter

Printed in Great Britain
by Amazon

22478857R00128